Praise for Macavity-winning author
BARB GOFFMAN

"Some say revenge is a dish best served cold,
but I'll take it cold, hot, or lukewarm as long as
it's served up by the talented Barb Goffman."
Bestselling author
TONI L.P. KELNER

"Each of these stories delivers a deft,
pleasing jolt. Barb Goffman is a fresh
voice in mystery fiction, but she brings
the skills of a seasoned veteran."
New York Times
bestselling author
DANIEL STASHOWER

DON'T GET MAD, GET EVEN

15 TALES OF REVENGE AND MORE

BARB GOFFMAN

To Mickey,
Happy reading.
Murder rocks!
Barb GoH

WILDSIDE PRESS

Published by Wildside Press, LLC
www.wildsidebooks.com

In honor of my dad,
who can always make me laugh.
And in memory of my sister-in-law Cyndi,
who left us way too soon.

CONTENTS

ACKNOWLEDGMENTS

This collection includes stories I wrote over the past decade, and the number of people who have helped me or influenced me during this time period is immense. Top in my mind are the authors from my critique groups, current and former: Donna Andrews, Tim Bentler-Jungr, Renee Brown, Erin Bush, Meriah Crawford, Sindy Felin, John Ford, C. Ellett Logan, Carolyn Mulford, Mary Nelson, Jack O'Donnell, Helen Schwartz, Shelley Shearer, Sylvia Straub, and Laura Weatherly.

Thank you to all my family and friends who have provided encouragement and assistance. Thank you to Noreen Wald, who taught my first mystery-writing class and made me think my writing was good when (looking back on it now) it really wasn't. Thank you to Marcia Talley, who reached out to me several years ago and told me I should be writing novels—that was a real confidence booster. Thank you to my friends in Sisters in Crime, especially my friends in my local Chesapeake Chapter, who have always had my back. And thank you to Carla Coupe and John Betancourt at Wildside Press, who surprised me last year, saying they wanted to publish a collection of my stories. That was one of the best days of my life.

Finally, I give special thanks to Donna Andrews, who encouraged (okay, nagged) me to get back into writing when I had stopped with one published story under my belt. This collection would not exist if not for her.

NIGHTMARE

Smoke stung my eyes as I scrambled back against my headboard. The dragon kept coming, its nostrils breathing fire. Closer and closer. Its orange tongue lashed out, stinging my stomach. Searing it. I kicked and screamed. Tears blurred my vision. But the dragon kept scalding me over and over, while my skin bubbled in waves of pain. "No," I yelled. Then I heard a thump.

I awoke with a start to the clap of thunder. Rain pelted against the roof, loud as a thousand marbles spilling onto the floor. I lay panting, snared in my twisted top sheet, drenched with sweat. The overhead fan whirling round and round flapped my summer babysitting schedule against my bulletin board, but did nothing to cool me. I could practically gulp the air.

Wrenching myself from my damp sheet, I tumbled out of bed and walked to the window, looking for…I didn't know what. I couldn't see anything in the backyard. The clouds had blocked the stars. Rain and a heavy breeze gusted in through the screen, raising goose bumps on my bare arms. I shivered despite the heat and shut the window.

I switched on my bedside lamp and tugged off my cami. Squinting, I rummaged through the clothes on the floor and pulled on shorts and one of my softball shirts. As I turned back to shut off the light, I elbowed a framed photo sitting on my bookshelf. It tipped backward, clinking against the one behind it before sliding onto the shelf with an even louder clang. I held my breath, listening, hoping I hadn't woken Mama.…Nothing. Relieved, I picked up the picture. It was of Mama, Brady, and me, out to dinner last month, celebrating Brady's graduation from high school and mine from middle school. Brady sat between Mama and me at the table, arms circling us, pulling us close. It had been a fun night, with the waitress mentioning how much Brady and I looked alike, with our wavy black hair and high cheekbones. How much we looked like Daddy.

I set that frame aside and picked up the dusty one behind it. It was of Mama and Daddy, a long time ago, back when she wore her auburn hair in a pixie cut. Daddy had his arm around her, his yellowed fingers squeezing her shoulder. I barely remembered Daddy. He ran off when I was six. Mama must have really loved him, though, because I couldn't recall her ever looking at another man all these years.

I turned off the lamp and tiptoed out to our front porch, trying not to wake Mama or Brady. The swing cushion was damp from the mist, but I sat anyway. It was the second time tonight I'd curled up on the swing. The first time had been before I turned in, before the skies had opened. I had swayed for nearly an hour then, pushing the air around to the chorus of frogs in the nearby creek, wishing a cooling rain would finally come. Or that Mama would give in and buy us an air conditioner. That had been when Brady drove up after his evening shift at the 7-Eleven. He'd climbed out of Mama's old pickup and stood by the truck door, a dark orange light flickering beside his face. I'd scooted back hard, trembling as I gripped the seat cushion. When had Brady started smoking? Mama wouldn't like that one bit. As the overhead light in the pickup had begun to fade, Brady flicked the butt onto the gravel drive, swept rocks over it with his foot, and headed inside. I had sat quietly in the dark the whole time, breathing fast, hoping he wouldn't notice me. I figured he didn't want me in on his big secret.

Now, a few hours later, the rain had come, and I was gliding on the swing once more. I eased it back and forth, listening to the downpour as my thoughts flitted between Brady smoking and the dream I'd just had. The dragon coming at me. Closer and closer. I hadn't thought about that dragon in years, though the nightmare had been a regular feature of my childhood.

Another clap of thunder shook the house. And shook my memories free.

* * * *

A half hour later, both my heart rate and the rain had slowed. I crept inside for my tennis shoes and a flashlight before going to the shed. Mama's gardening gloves were right where I expected. I shoved them in my pocket. Then, shaking off raindrops sliding down my forehead, I pulled out a shovel.

The ground was soft as I trudged to the far corner of our property, each step like walking through a steam room. I stopped when I reached the big oak tree that I often lay against on hot summer days, drinking Mama's lemonade and squishing my toes in the grass while I read under its protective shade. I patted the rough bark. That tree had always given me comfort.

I picked the lowest branch closest to the house and stepped beneath its tip. This seemed the right spot. I took a deep breath, the smell of the grass reminding me of my grandparents' farm on mowing days. I shut off the flashlight and began digging, grateful there was no lightning tonight. Hoping none would come.

The earth gave way easily enough thanks to the storm. I dug for a while, my muscles appreciating the repetitive motion. The rain was much lighter now. Still, droplets snuck into my hair and wound down my back. And drizzle mixed with sweat pasted my bangs to my forehead. Wishing I'd pulled my hair into a ponytail, I paused to mop my face with my shirt. Then I continued digging.

It took longer than I'd expected. Finally the shovel hit something solid. I tugged on the garden gloves, fell to my knees, and began scooping away the dirt. Faster and faster. Soon I leaned back. I knew what I'd reached, but I clicked on the flashlight to be sure.

Bones—a lot of large ones—with a belt buckle, a pipe, and a lighter.

Daddy's lighter. Red with a picture of a crown on the side.

I swallowed hard. So the memories were real, not just my imagination working overtime.

"You shouldn't be out here, Mary Ellen."

I stood and turned, aiming the flashlight at Brady's feet so not to blind him. I hadn't heard him come up, yet I wasn't surprised to see him. Brady could walk like a ghost. As he had that night he saved me from Daddy. I blinked a few times, unable to tell if the water on my cheeks came from my eyes or the sky.

"And you shouldn't smoke, Brady."

"I thought I saw you on the porch when I got home." He sighed. "A nasty habit, all right. After Daddy, you'd think I'd never touch a cigarette, but..." He shrugged.

I nodded. I'd keep my brother, warts and all. Mama had been upset when Brady insisted on going to our community college this fall and living at home instead of attending a better school across state. But I'd been thrilled.

"Would you get the other shovel and help me rebury Daddy before anyone notices? We've got another hour or so before sun-up."

He reached out and gently stroked my arm. My arm, with the little round burn marks. Mama had said they came from a kitchen accident when I was real young. But she never explained the ones on my stomach and thighs.

Quickly Brady grabbed the other shovel and together we reburied the dragon. I was glad that this time, I got to do it myself instead of watching him and Mama from my bedroom window.

But...

"Brady," I said, as we were almost finished, "I don't remember Daddy smoking a pipe. Just cigarettes."

"He didn't. The guy who started sniffing around Mama after Daddy…left did. I told her this family would never need any man other than me."

Brady paused and stared at me hard with an odd kind of smile. The hair on my neck rose.

"You'll never need anyone other than me. Will you, Mary Ellen?"

❦

Sometimes I wake up in the middle of the night, hearing voices in my head. Characters fully developed, telling me their story. On good nights, I get up, grab a pen and paper, and write down what they say. That is how "Nightmare" was born. The thunderstorm. The swing. The cigarette. The southern-gothic feel. It all poured out of me in the middle of the night, a gift from my muse, and now my gift to you. "Nightmare" is the first of five new stories in this collection. I hope you enjoy all the tales in this book as much as I've loved writing them.

BON APPÉTIT

Another gust of wind rattled the window frames. I shivered as Jenny pulled the photo album closer and pointed at a wedding snapshot of Dwayne, Larry, and me. Dwayne didn't have any of the stubble or anger that usually graced his face these days. Grinning widely, like a kid who'd gotten two desserts, he stood in his rented tux with one arm around my bare, freckled shoulders and the other around my brother, Larry's, broad ones. It was a fitting pose, considering how Dwayne ultimately came between Larry and me. I hadn't seen my brother in twenty years.

"Look how skinny you were." Jenny brushed her curly brown hair from her eyes.

I shifted my chair closer to my scarred kitchen table and laughed. "Yep. Those were the days." Back before Dwayne began hitting me. Before I told Larry about it. Before he nearly beat Dwayne to death and went to prison for it. Hard time up at Macon. Dwayne wouldn't let me visit him. Ever. At least Larry and I wrote letters, and sometimes he called.

Jenny leaned back, trying to smile, but the corners of her mouth kept tugging down. "I love you, you know."

My eyes watered. "I love you, too."

Jenny had been my best friend ever since Dwayne and I moved here to Willacoochee. She lived on a small farm a mile up the road with her husband, four children, and two hound dogs. Nearly every day we were in and out of each other's kitchens, sharing flour and vegetables and smiles. If I was going to miss anyone, it would be Jenny, though I guess once you're dead, you can't miss anyone or anything.

I stood and picked up a ceramic plate off the counter. It had sunflowers on it—Mama's favorite—just like the ones I grew in my garden. I'd made the plate for Mama for her birthday next month, but that day was never going to come now. "I want you to have this." I held the plate out to Jenny. "I know how much you like it."

"Are you sure?"

"Yep. Besides Mama, you're the only one who ever supported my crafts."

Jenny sniffed as she ran her fingers over the sunflowers, their warmth and brightness a sad reminder of better days. "Dwayne's a fool, you know."

Oh, I knew. Early in my marriage, I'd dreamed of opening my own shop and selling my work, but Dwayne had made it clear that was never going to happen. Running a store was too costly, he'd said. Too risky. "You don't have it in you to make a store succeed, Violet. Now focus on what you're good at and make me a pie."

"Have you been able to reach your mother?" Jenny asked, bringing me back to the present.

"I finally got through to Aunt Sarah's this morning. It's been so hard with the phone lines being jammed all the time. I've only received one call all week." I leaned against the counter and sighed, grateful that Aunt Sarah had taken Mama in when she got sick, after Dwayne refused to let her live with us. "Mama's Alzheimer's has gotten worse. She didn't even recognize my voice."

"I'm sorry. I'm so glad I got to see my whole family last week. It makes all this easier."

Her voice started to break. I hugged her.

"Well, at least you won't have to worry about cooking any more big Thanksgiving meals," I said, trying to lighten the mood. But it didn't work. It's hard to joke when an enormous comet is set to hit the earth in a few hours, ending all life. That's how they phrased it on the news last night. Ending all life.

I pulled away and turned on the lights, thankful once again for our generator. It had been getting darker all day. The shadows stretching across the floor made it look more like late evening than mid-afternoon.

Jenny wiped unshed tears from her eyes. "What are you making for your last meal?"

"Steaks. I've been saving them for a special occasion. I guess the end of the world qualifies." I swallowed hard. "And I'm making mashed potatoes with lots of butter, just like Mama used to. Everyone's always loved them."

"Especially me." Jenny patted her stomach. "Well, I guess I better get home. The kids want their favorite oatmeal cookies, and they're not going to bake themselves. Thanks for giving me the last of your brown sugar."

"Sure. It's not like I'll need it anymore."

Jenny and I had been sharing more and more food these last few weeks, ever since the government confirmed what the scientists had been saying for months and most of the stores had been picked clean and shut down. It made sense. Who'd want to spend their last days selling stuff when they could be with their families?

Jenny stepped toward the back door.

"Wait." I grabbed one of three pies I had cooling by the sink. "Take this. I made it for you from the last of my pickings."

"Blueberry. How can I resist?" Jenny lowered her nose to the lattice crust and breathed in. "Mmmm. I'm sure it will be delicious. You should have opened that bakery like we always talked about."

That had been another dream of mine. But Dwayne had reminded me I didn't have *that* in me either. Too much work, he'd said, for a woman who flits around the garden all day.

I hugged my best friend hard, and then, with a smile and a wave, she was gone.

I took a deep breath and checked my watch. Dwayne would be home soon enough, I realized. I'd best start preparing dinner. I turned on the TV for company. Most of the channels had gone dark weeks ago, but CNN was still running with a limited staff of die-hards who said they'd report to the bitter end.

"More and more people keep coming here to Central Park, joining the thousands who've been camping and singing songs," a reporter stationed in New York City said. "It's a lot different from the reports we've been hearing out of Seattle and L.A., where the riots are ongoing."

The camera switched back to the blond anchor. "Thanks for that report, Mark. In other news, a warden in Oregon released his prisoners this morning after ninety-nine percent of state employees, including prison guards, failed to report to work, leaving the prisons with no way to supervise or provide food to the inmates. This is the third such report we've had this week, following releases in Georgia and West Virginia. All three wardens said it would be inhumane to house prisoners under such conditions."

Outside, the shutters started slapping against the house, and the wind began to whistle. They'd said the weather would continue to worsen as the end grew near. I pushed aside the white curtains covering the window over the sink. The sky was growing darker still. I fretted for a few seconds, then pulled myself together. This was no time to go to pieces. I had work to do.

* * * *

A couple hours later the vegetables were picked, washed, and chopped, the potatoes were peeled, and the steaks were tenderized and ready to go. I stood at the window, glancing at the road as I finished making a cucumber salad using the last of my crop. Then, behind me, I heard the back screen door bang against the frame. My breath caught.

"That's what I like to see." Dwayne's words ran into one another. "My little woman cooking for me, even today."

I sighed, my shoulders slumping. He must have stumbled in from over the hill out back. I began turning, but Dwayne crossed the room quicker than I expected and squeezed me from behind, rubbing his hands over my chest, and grinding his pelvis into the back of my dress.

"You smell nice," he said.

"And you smell like a brewery." I wrenched away from him and turned. "You said you were going to spend today fishing. Looks like you spent it at Gus's instead."

Dwayne's brown eyes narrowed. I shouldn't have said that, especially not with that tone. Complaints like that usually pissed Dwayne off and made him come after me. But I couldn't help myself. This was going to be our last night together, yet he came home with the lingering stench of that swill Gus brewed. Did Dwayne actually think I'd want to spend my last hours on this earth having sex with him when he smelled like he'd fallen into a vat of rancid beer? Oh, who was I kidding? Dwayne never cared what I wanted.

"Why's everything always a fight with you?"

He grabbed my arm and yanked me toward the bedroom. I was thankful it would be the last time I'd have to put up with him. I just hoped he'd be quick as always.

* * * *

"Jesus. Aren't those steaks done yet? I'm hungry."

Dwayne had finished his afternoon *delight* pretty quick and fallen asleep. Now, after an hour's nap, he'd parked himself at the kitchen table and was two beers into his last six-pack.

"Don't you like the salad?"

He pushed the plate away. A cherry tomato rolled onto the floor. "What's the point of eating healthy anymore? We're all gonna die tonight anyway."

He had a point there. My frying pan sizzled as I sprinkled minced garlic over the mushrooms. The savory fragrance wafted around me. "Dinner's almost ready, and I made a nice peach pie for dessert with extra sugar on top."

Dwayne grunted. Given that this was his last meal, I'd wanted to make a dessert he'd tuck into with fervor, so I'd chosen peach filling—his favorite—and added the sugar to make it especially enticing.

"I was talking with Jenny today," I said, adding evaporated milk to the potatoes. "She reminded me how much I like cooking for people. I should have opened that bakery when I had the chance."

Now Dwayne snorted. "Not that crap again, Violet. You'd never have been able to pull something like that off. You don't have it in you."

I growled under my breath as I began to beat the potatoes. How many times had I let him discourage me with those demeaning words? The back screen door slammed against its frame again, but it was only the wind. It had really picked up. I blew out a deep breath. Just a few hours left. At least I wouldn't have to listen to Dwayne's put-downs anymore.

I dished the mashed potatoes onto our plates, then the steaks, my large frying pan sputtering as I pulled it off the stove for the last time. Then I poured the garlic and mushrooms on top of Dwayne's steak. I'd never cared for mushrooms, but he enjoyed them.

"Here you go." I set the plates down on the table and settled into my chair, facing Dwayne. Behind him, the back door rattled. The sky looked black and daunting through the door's window, but the warm yellow porch light gave me comfort.

Dwayne picked up his knife and fork and dug in.

"I flipped through some photo albums today," I said. "You remember how much fun our wedding was?"

I got no response other than slurping and chewing noises. You'd think given that it was his last meal, Dwayne would savor the food, but he was shoveling it in.

So I gave up on conversation and sipped my sweet tea between forkfuls of salad, steak, and mashed potatoes. How Larry had loved Mama's potatoes. He always ate ravenously, too, but at least he told good stories between bites, like the one about the boy who grew up near us who loved to wander the countryside. He came home one day with real bad stomach cramps. Thank goodness his family rushed him to the hospital. Turned out he'd eaten some poisonous mushrooms. You've got to be real careful about what you pick in the woods.

Soon enough, Dwayne practically licked his plate clean. He popped open another beer and said, "Where's that dessert you promised?"

I still had half my dinner remaining, but why should that matter to him? I got up from the table to serve his highness. I sliced an extra large piece of the peach pie and brought it to Dwayne. "*Bon appétit.*"

I sat back down and decided to make another stab at conversation. "My garden has really come in handy these last couple months. We haven't had to worry about food, unlike some city folks I've seen on the news. Even tonight, with our last meal, everything's fresh."

"Another reason why it's good to live in the country," Dwayne said while chewing. Then he set down his fork and touched his stomach.

"Everything okay?" I took another bite of my potatoes. They had come out just right.

"A little indigestion. Guess I ate too fast."

"Well then, take a breather. That pie'll sit."

I heard a snap, then the roof shook. Sounded like a large branch had crashed onto it. I went to the back door and looked out the window, but I couldn't see anything or anyone.

"Dwayne, are you scared?" I asked as I resumed my seat.

"Not worth being scared, Violet. What's gonna happen is gonna happen. I plan to drink the rest of this beer and be sound asleep when that old comet hits. You remember how my daddy died in his sleep. It's the best way to go."

Yes, I supposed it would be.

Dwayne lifted up another bite of pie, brought it toward his mouth, then started looking peaked. He dropped the fork and ran to the bathroom. Soon I heard him losing his meal. A small smile crept across my face as I kept eating mine.

"You sure you're all right?" I asked when he finally returned to the kitchen. He was pale and clutching his stomach. He tumbled into his chair, grimaced at his remaining pie, and pushed the plate away.

"Jesus, Violet. My last meal and you gave me food poisoning." He began moaning and put his head down on the table.

"Nope. There is no bacteria in this food. You know how careful I am with my cooking." I finished the last of my steak. Delicious.

Dwayne ran back to the bathroom. He was in there a while, losing more of his meal from both ends, apparently, as I cleared the dishes. When he finally came back to the table, sweating and breathing hard, he looked like death. Of course, death was a few hours off. I didn't know if he'd die from the comet or those special mushrooms or the little something extra I'd added to the pie. Either way, before his end came, Dwayne would spend his last hours suffering.

As he should.

He slumped back in his chair and started moaning again.

"Maybe you caught a bug, Dwayne. My meal tasted just right." I took my seat at the table and looked at the wildflowers I'd gathered that morning, sitting in a vase on the counter. They were so much nicer than Dwayne's scrunched-up face. "Or maybe it was those mushrooms you ate." I looked him square on now. "I picked them just for you."

He stared at me, eyes wide. "What did you do?"

Dwayne lurched at me. I clenched my jaw and scooted my chair back, but before Dwayne could reach me he groaned loudly and fell to the floor, grabbing at his stomach.

"Cramps?" I asked.

He didn't answer. Just kept lying there, moaning and writhing and gasping for breath, while the wind howled outside and the back porch began to creak.

Suddenly the back door screeched opened. A man with long, messy brown hair walked in. His face was lined and craggy, and his nose was off center, but his eyes were as sharp as ever. Larry.

I jumped up, ran around the table (stepping on Dwayne's hand—oops), and hugged my brother. Oh, how I'd missed him. And how grateful I was to that warden who'd let him out.

When I pulled back, Larry rubbed my cheek, then looked over my shoulder and began shaking his head and laughing.

"Dwayne's dinner didn't quite agree with him." I smiled. "Would you please carry him out on the porch? All his moaning is getting on my nerves."

Larry scooped Dwayne up as if he weighed nothing. When Larry came back inside, I was slicing up the second blueberry pie I'd made that morning. Larry looked at the peach pie I'd thrown in the trash.

"Oh, you don't want that. I made it special for Dwayne. It has some Comet and other cleansers in it, in honor of our impending doom."

"Nice touch." Larry chuckled. "But why'd you do it? I told you when I called that I'd get here by tonight and would take care of him for you."

I paused and let out a deep sigh. "I appreciate that. But after everything Dwayne put me through, I decided I was going to stand up for myself, once and for all."

"Good for you, Sis. I always knew you had it in you."

I nearly laughed at his wording. "Thanks, Larry. I just wish I'd known it sooner."

We sat at the table with our pie and old photo albums. The wind howled again, but I didn't mind anymore. I finally had my big brother back, if only for a few hours.

❄

"Bon Appétit" first appeared in Nightfalls: Notes From the End of the World, *published by Dark Valentine Press in 2012.*

This story was a bit of a challenge. The editor of Nightfalls, *Katherine Tomlinson, asked me to submit to the anthology. Every story in the book would be set on the night before the world was going to end. Katherine wanted to see how people would spend that night, knowing their time was definitely limited. That set-up might prove easier to authors of romance, I thought. I write crime. If the world were ending, certain crimes would become obsolete. Money wouldn't matter anymore, so that ruled out stories about burglaries and robberies. Terrorism would probably be out, too, since the world already was doomed. I thought and thought, and ultimately I realized that in the end, all you have is love and self-respect. Oh yeah, and revenge. Definitely revenge. And "Bon Appétit" was born.*

THE WORST NOEL

Okay, Gwen. Get ready to fake it.

It was nearly my turn to share what I was thankful for. Then we'd eat some pie, Thanksgiving dinner would mercifully end, and I could escape for home.

But first I had to pay my annual homage to Mom, saying how thankful I am for my family. Every year I contemplate only mentioning my friends and work, but I always chicken out. Mom would make me pay if I didn't smile and mention her.

My sister, Becca, finally stopped blathering about her husband and baby, and Mom slipped into the kitchen, clearly satisfied, as always, with Becca.

Becca's husband, Joe, started sharing his thanks. I reached for another roll, slathered some butter on it, and swallowed it down in two bites. Joe finished talking. I steeled myself. My turn had come. I smiled and—

"Happy birthday to you," Mom sang, emerging from the kitchen with a large pumpkin pie, a candle in the middle. Everyone joined in, Becca's in-laws looking uncomfortable, while Mom set the pie before me.

"We would have wished you happy birthday earlier," Joe said, glancing at his parents when the song ended. "But we thought your birthday was tomorrow."

"Oh, it is," Mom piped in. "But Becca and I will be busy shopping, so it only makes sense to celebrate Gwen's birthday now."

I wished I had a different family and blew out my candle.

"Pumpkin pie as birthday cake," Joe said. "How unusual."

He knew my preference for chocolate. As did Mom.

"Well, it is Thanksgiving. Besides"—Mom poked me with her elbow—"it's not like Gwen needs any more cake." She smiled as if she hadn't just been incredibly rude to me. "Becca, would you please slice the pie? I'm going to get Gwen's gift."

A couple minutes later, as plates of pie made the rounds and I considered dropping mine, face down, on Mom's Berber carpet, Mom handed me a gold-wrapped box. I opened the envelope first, and a small gift card fell out. I turned it over and cringed. Not a gift card. A membership card. For a gym.

This was a new low, even for Mom.

"Read the greeting card," she said.

Lord save me. "To our darling daughter on her birthday," I read aloud. Not that Mom or Dad had penned that sentiment. It came straight from Hallmark. At the bottom, Mom had written, "We got you this gym membership and a personal trainer for the next six months. Happy Birthday."

Oh, yeah. There's nothing like being reminded that you're fat to make your birthday a humdinger!

"What a wonderful gift," Becca said in that tone she'd used since we were kids—the one grown-ups always thought sounded sweet and sincere but I knew was chockfull of sarcasm.

"There's more!" Mom said, pointing at the box, looking proud.

I shuddered to imagine what might be in it. I gingerly opened the gold wrapping paper, not because I cared about ripping it, but because I wanted to delay every second I could before the inevitable torture.

Paper off, the box's lid caught my eye. Bloomingdale's. Really? Excited, I lifted off the cover, pulled back the crinkly, white tissue paper, and...mentally kicked myself for thinking Mom might have gotten me something nice.

"Hold it up," Mom said. "Let everyone see."

I pulled out my gift. A red sweat suit. Size medium.

"You can use it at the gym! With the trainer!" she said.

I watched Becca try not to laugh while her in-laws and Joe sat there, mouths open.

"Thank you, Mom. Dad. How very…thoughtful."

"Go try it on," Mom said.

"Oh, no, not right now."

"C'mon, Gwen," Becca chimed in. "Don't be shy. Let's see how it looks."

I glared at her. She knew damn well how it would look.

Mom gave me her don't-embarrass-me frown. So I shuffled off to my old bedroom, sweat suit in hand. As an elementary school principal, I'm used to standing up to people and holding my own. But you wouldn't know it seeing me around my family. While I took off my clothes, I wondered for the millionth time why Mom and Dad favored Becca so much. Growing up, they had always given her great presents. First the hottest toys, then trendy teenage clothes, and then expensive jewelry from Cartier in Boston. Oh, how she'd always loved to laud her gifts over me.

Especially since my presents always sucked. When I turned eight, Cabbage Patch dolls were all the rage. I got a Skipper doll. Mom wouldn't even spring for Barbie. At fourteen, I begged for bohemian clothes from Annie Dakota, a funky store that used to be downtown. I got a science tutor instead. "A far better use of the money," Mom had said, looking me up and down. "We can't count on you finding a husband like Becca surely will, and I don't want to have to support you for the rest of my life." Becca had snickered while my few friends whom I'd invited over for cake gasped—they'd heard my stories about Mom, but nothing shocked like seeing her in action.

Given the history, I shouldn't have been surprised by today's events. And yet a tiny part of me hoped every year that things would be different. Stupid, stupid, stupid.

I struggled to get the sweat suit on, tugging the snug pants over my hips and fighting to pull the top's zipper over my bosom. When I finally finished and peered in the mirror, I cringed. The red sweat suit had a white collar and cuffs. I looked like a pregnant Santa Claus.

"What's taking so long, Gwen?" Mom called from the hall. "If you don't come out right now, I'm just going to come in on my own."

I opened the door, Mom sucked in her breath, and Becca burst out laughing.

"I'll have to return it." I gestured at the red nightmare. "It's a bit tight."

"Of course it's tight." Mom rolled her eyes. "How will you ever be encouraged to lose weight if you constantly wear fat clothes? That's why I bought you a medium."

Tears welled up in my eyes, but I wouldn't let them flow.

Mom clapped her hands together. "That's enough about you, Gwen. This is a holiday for the whole family, after all, and we have guests. Get dressed and come back and join everyone."

"Wait." Becca handed me another box. "This is from me and Joe. But you don't have to model it now. I'm sure it'll look great on you."

Right. I closed the door and sank onto my old bed, the springs creaking. Sighing, I opened Becca's gift. A royal blue sweater with horizontal white stripes. At least it was the right size, but stripes! It would look hideous on me. Of course it didn't come as a surprise. Every year since we'd become adults, Becca had given me gifts that made me look bad. In return, every year I'd bought her gifts she wouldn't like. Last year, a bargain-brand video camera. This year, a silver bracelet. Becca only wears gold.

I looked at my watch. How soon could I leave without Mom calling me rude? Whatever the time, it wouldn't be soon enough.

* * * *

Two Saturdays later Hanukkah was set to begin, and once again, I had to deal with my family. Mom demanded we celebrate the first night at my place this year, which was unusual. Since Dad was the only real Jewish person in our immediate family—Becca and I had been raised Presbyterian, like Mom, but with a fine appreciation for the gift-oriented Jewish holidays—we always celebrated the first night of Hanukkah at Mom and Dad's. Odder still was Mom's insistence on coming over early in the afternoon. Hanukkah didn't start until sundown, and I couldn't imagine Mom really wanted to hang out for several hours in my rented townhouse in my "bad" neighborhood.

Still, shortly after lunch, Mom and Dad arrived. Mom made a beeline for my Christmas tree. She stood silent, arms folded, studying it. I had just strung up the colored lights and a few glittering ornaments the night before. It looked great.

"Honestly, Gwen," Mom finally said. "Why must you pick the scruffiest, most pathetic tree every year? It's like you try to embarrass me." She walked over to the window and pulled the curtains closed so the neighbors wouldn't have to suffer seeing my tree.

Stung, I went downstairs to take some deep breaths and dig out my menorah. I found no leftover candles. Fabulous! I could escape to the market to buy a box. I'd need two candles for tonight, three for tomorrow, and so on for the eight nights of Hanukkah. I always liked saying the prayers and lighting the candles. It made me feel peaceful.

Focusing on staying calm, I returned to the living room, and my eyes nearly bugged out. Mom was directing two delivery men to move my love seat to a corner and set a big box in its place.

"What's going on?" I asked.

"Surprise!" Mom waved her hand at the box like the girls from The Price is Right do. "Happy Hanukkah." She nodded at the workmen, and they pulled apart the box to reveal...oh, my Lord. A treadmill. "It's for snowy days when you can't get to the gym this winter," she said.

I felt a major migraine coming on, and I never got migraines.

I stood dumbfounded while the workmen set up the tread-mill. I still hadn't said a word by the time they left.

"Don't give me that look, Gwen," Mom said. "Once I saw that sweat suit on you, I knew you wouldn't wear it out of the house. Now you have no excuse not to put it on. Come, Henry, let's go home and give Gwen a chance to try out her present."

"What?" I shook my head. "What about lighting the candles tonight?"

Mom scrunched her eyebrows, confused. "We're not actually going to do that here, Gwen. We'll light the candles at home, as always. I'll expect you before sundown." She pushed Dad toward the door, then turned to look at the treadmill. "And by the way, you're welcome."

* * * *

The next night, after lighting the candles at home, I thought back to Thanksgiving and realized I now had something family-oriented to be thankful for. I wouldn't have to see Mom or Becca for three whole weeks, when we'd all have Christmas Eve dinner at Becca's.

I had twenty-one blissful, family-free days to look forward to. Happy, I wrote some holiday cards to old friends while a batch of sugar cookies baked in the oven.

My happiness didn't last long. The next morning, Mom showed up at my school. She'd never expressed any interest in my job before. I had just finished meeting with a parent and was showing her out when Mom practically swaggered into the school office.

"Gwen," she interrupted. "I have the most fantastic news!"

Please be moving to Florida.

Mom looked around until she was sure she had the attention of the secretaries, my vice-principal, and a student who was in the room, as well as the departing parent and myself. Then she clapped her hands together. "Your brother-in-law, the doctor," she said, emphasizing the word, like I didn't know Joe's profession, "has been chosen to play a very prominent rebel in the next Patriots' Day re-enactment."

Wow. I had grown up in nearby Lexington, home of the American Revolution, and its Patriots' Day re-enactment each April was a big deal around here. Being asked to play any important position was a great honor for Joe, who deserved it both for being a nice guy and for putting up with my sister.

Everyone oohed and ahhed appropriately. Mom beamed.

"Your sister certainly hit the jackpot with her husband," she said, picking lint off my suit jacket. "It's such a shame you don't have a man in your life, darling. Or any prospects. Maybe if you actually used that treadmill..."

I looked for a hole in the floor to crawl into.

"Anyway," Mom continued. "Becca is planning a family celebration at her home Friday night at eight. You're expected to attend."

With a quick nod, Mom walked out. Everyone in the office turned away, embarrassed, and I felt something in me break.

It was one thing for Mom to belittle me in front of friends and family. That I'd grown used to. But now she'd polluted my work environment. Undermined my authority. And thrown Becca in my face. Again.

Escaping my colleagues' pitying glances, I went to my private office and paced.

Becca always got everything, yet she was such a witch. Joe and my nephew, Charlie, would be so much better off without her.

And Mom. She claimed to love me, but she only really loved herself—and Becca.

In a flash, a plan unfolded in my mind. So simple. I could kill both birds with one stone.

Well...I wouldn't actually kill them both.

* * * *

As soon as school let out that afternoon, I headed over to Becca's. I gushed over Joe's news and the tasteful, all-white Christmas lights they had strung up outside. (I always liked the multi-colored ones myself.) Then I suggested Becca model the suede coat Mom had bought her for Hanukkah. On her way to the closet, Becca made a snide comment about my treadmill. I let it go—and swiped her spare house key.

A little later I drove to the hospital where Joe works for advice on what to get Becca for Christmas. In the few minutes he could spare to chat, Joe left his office twice to deal with patient issues. As I'd hoped. He was only gone a minute or so each time, but long enough for me to find his prescription pad and rip off a sheet. On the way out of the hospital, I passed a drug cart helpfully left alone in a hallway. I swiped some random pills and hurried out. That evening, I had a copy of Becca's house key made. Everything was falling into place.

When school let out the next afternoon, I returned to Becca's. I knew the house would be empty, Charlie with his nanny at a Mommy and Me class, Joe at work, and Becca out playing mahjong. I wiped down her key and put it back. Then I went into her study, got on the Internet, and ordered some OxyContin using Becca's email and credit card number (so helpful that Joe filed all the bills neatly in a desk cabinet). Then I faxed in my fake prescription. My handwriting didn't look anything like Joe's, but that didn't matter. What was important was my handwriting looked like Becca's.

Come Friday morning, I called in sick. But I was actually feeling giddy. Knowing Joe was at work and Charlie would be at the park with the nanny, I phoned Becca and told her about great Christmas sales going on at Macy's and Lord and Taylor. She actually thanked me and raced out.

I headed over to her house, parking down the street so the neighbors wouldn't notice my car, and let myself in. While I waited for the drugs (I paid extra for delivery by 11 a.m.), I played around in Becca's cabinets, switching salt for sugar, that type of thing. When my package finally came, I shoved the receipt in the back of a drawer and went home, only to return a few hours later for Joe's dinner.

I felt a little bad about ruining his celebration, but it couldn't be helped. It was especially nice that Mom had invited one of her friends from the National Heritage Museum to dinner at Becca's to show Joe off. Now I'd have a witness to the tension between Mom and Becca.

Priceless is the best way to describe everyone's faces, especially Mom's, as they tasted the supposedly sweet and sour chicken that was actually salty and bitter. Becca's mouth hung open. She'd always prided herself on being the perfect cook and hostess.

"I'm sorry," she said. "I can't imagine what went wrong. Please have more of the salad and rolls." She hurried into the kitchen to try to pull something else together. Mom followed her.

"If you didn't have time to cook a proper dinner, Becca, you should have told me," Mom said in her usual whisper that could be heard in the next township. "You've embarrassed me. I typically count on Gwen for that."

Before Becca could defend herself, Mom emerged from the kitchen, a tight smile on her face. "Madeline." She nodded to her friend. "Why don't we go out for a proper meal? It's on us, of course."

In seconds Mom, Dad, and Madeline headed for the door, while Becca shot daggers from her eyes at Mom's back. I was so happy, Mom's jab at me hardly registered.

I went home soon after, singing "Jingle Bells" and feeling quite merry indeed.

* * * *

On Sunday, the first flurries of the season came. I watched them happily through the window at a cute café near my townhouse where I was having lunch with Aunt Lynn, Dad's sister. I waited for her to mention Becca, and when she finally did, I said, "Mom's being so hard on Becca since she put on those ten pounds."

"What ten pounds? The girl's a stick."

"I know. You certainly can't tell by looking at her. But you know Mom."

Aunt Lynn did know Mom, very well. (It's why she made plans with other relatives every Thanksgiving.) She shook her head, the tiny diamonds on the Jewish star around her neck sparkling in the light. "That woman. One day someone's going to put her in her place."

"I'm surprised Becca didn't tell Mom off herself. I guess she's too embarrassed about the weight gain. I don't think she's confided in anyone but the two of us. So don't say anything."

Aunt Lynn crossed her heart. I knew I could count on her keeping her word. Well, at least until the police came asking.

* * * *

Finally, Christmas Eve day came. I headed over to Becca's shortly after breakfast. I knew she and Joe planned to take Charlie to the mall for a final chance to see Santa before the line got too long. They'd actually given their nanny a couple days off.

I also knew that this afternoon Becca would make lemon torte, Mom's favorite, for dessert. Wearing gloves, I opened the pantry, and into each of the ingredients, I mixed some of the stolen pills and OxyContin. I didn't know what the pills would do, but I figured the OxyContin would kill Mom, and if she suffered from the other ground-up medicines, all the better.

And—the topper—Becca would be blamed. Her inevitable refusal to eat the high-calorie dessert, coupled with the

OxyContin billed to her credit card, would guarantee it, just in case the police had any doubt.

I spent the afternoon baking and watching *It's a Wonderful Life*. As it ended, I became melancholy. Was I being too hard on Mom and Becca? Heading to the kitchen for brownies to help me think, I stubbed my toe on the damn treadmill. All the anger and memories flooded back. No, I wasn't being too hard on them. Not by a long shot. They had brought this on themselves.

I arrived a little later at Becca's, armed with presents, and happily learned Joe had to work tonight in order to get Christmas day off. It would be much better without a doctor in the house. Becca had already fed Charlie and put him to bed. So it was just Mom, Dad, Becca, and me for dinner. Our small, happy family.

The first two courses went swimmingly for Becca. Mom fawned over her shrimp puff appetizer and declared her main course of leg of lamb with roasted potatoes and steamed asparagus "simply divine." I was so excited, I helped myself to a couple extra rolls, along with a second helping of potatoes.

Finally it was time for dessert. Becca emerged from the kitchen with a small lemon torte. Mom narrowed her eyes. "Becca, why is this dish so small? There's hardly enough for two here, let alone four."

"I'm on a diet," she said. Shocking. "And Dad never eats lemon torte. I figured you and Gwen could share it. Dad and I can have cranberry yogurt."

Mom turned to me. "Well, Gwen. I know you never pass up dessert. Hand me your plate."

Oh, she so deserved what was coming. "Actually, I'm on a diet, too. You'll have to enjoy the lemon torte by yourself."

"A diet? I had no idea," Becca said. "And here I baked you a special, extra dessert to make up for that striped monstrosity I gave you for your birthday." She scurried into the kitchen and reappeared moments later with cranberry yogurt for her and Dad, and a large slice of fudge cake for me. My favorite.

"You made that?" I asked.

"Okay, you got me. It took a long time to bake the lemon torte, so I picked this up from that gourmet bakery down on Bedford Street. It's still good."

It looked better than good. "Well, since you went to all that trouble." I smiled and dug in. Then I leaned back in my chair while I watched Mom eat her dessert with her typical small, dainty bites.

"Becca, this is wonderful," Mom said, her face a bit flushed. "But it tastes different than it usually does. Did you change your recipe?"

"That's weird," she said. "I didn't change a thing. Gwen, how's your dessert?"

Now it was my turn to think things were weird. Becca appeared flushed, too. So did Dad. In fact everything seemed blotchy and out of focus. I shook my head, which made things worse. My stomach cramped, my head spun.

"Gwen," Becca said, "are you all right?"

I blinked and tried to answer, but I couldn't speak. Gasping for breath, I slumped to the floor. I was sweating yet felt so cold.

"Damn it, Gwen," I heard Mom say. "I told you to lose weight!" My eyes fluttered open. She was leaning over me. "Becca, call 911."

"It'll be faster if we drive to the hospital," Becca said. "It's started to snow. They're probably busy with accidents."

"Henry, go start the car!" Mom yelled.

"Mom." Becca knelt beside me as I began to shake. "Grab a blanket from the spare bedroom for Gwen!"

"Of course." She ran off.

Becca shifted closer. "I told a little fib earlier. I bought Mom's lemon torte from the bakery. I made your dessert from scratch."

I opened my eyes wide—the only movement I could make.

"That's right, Gwen. I can be crafty, too. Like how I've used that video camera you gave me last year. I set it up at first to spy on the nanny. Imagine my surprise these past few weeks, seeing you come and go." She sighed. "I'll look at today's tape next week and discover that you tampered with ingredients in my kitchen this morning. I'll tearfully hand it over to the cops and let them figure out that you...did yourself in."

I began wheezing. Dad ran over and, straining, lifted me up. While he carried me to the door, I saw Becca smile. Then I spied the Christmas gifts I'd put under the tree, and I smiled, too.

My back-up plan.

I felt peaceful as I drifted away, thinking of the sweets I'd made Mom and Becca for Christmas.

❀

"The Worst Noel" originally appeared in The Gift of Murder, *published by Wolfmont Press in 2009. This story was nominated for the 2009 Agatha Award.*

I think this story went through more revisions than any other story I've ever written (except "Evil Little Girl," which has dogged me for years). The first draft was inspired by a call for stories using the word medium. I believe that editor was looking for stories with psychics and methods of communication and things like that. But when I heard "medium," I immediately thought of the size. I thought of someone never living up to her family's standards because she wasn't a medium. She never would be. But the story didn't really come together until I heard of another call for stories a year or so later from Editor Tony Burton of Wolfmont Press. He wanted crime stories set at the holidays, and things began to click. Mix a tortured, overweight woman and her family and the holidays? Oh yes, that's certainly a recipe for murder.

COMPULSIVE BUBBA

My husband could best be described in three words. Compulsive. Abusive. Bubba.

I knew he was compulsive when I married him. Back then, I liked it. Liked how he showed up at my door at the precise moment he'd promised with a red rose in hand. Liked how he always looked as if he'd just whipped his clothes off an ironing board.

Most of all, I liked that he hailed from the South. I'd spent my first ten years in Georgia. Never thought I'd live anywhere else till the day Daddy moved us to Michigan, then up and died in a whiteout on the highway. After Mama remarried and my step-daddy turned out to be a mean drunk, I dreamed of getting out and moving back home. Back South. But I never had the means to do it till Jimmy came along. He dangled marriage and a house in Virginia before my eyes, and I was hooked. The thought of leaving my bad memories and returning to my roots appealed to me mightily. Not to mention, considering what happened to Daddy, I looked forward to never shoveling snow again.

Little did I know.

First time Jimmy hit me, it was snowing. A soft snow, with flakes like little cotton balls raining down from heaven. I hadn't bothered to sweep our front walk before Jimmy came home from work that night. Back in Michigan, we didn't pay no mind to light dustings.

I heard him muttering as the front door opened. His pants were wet, face red.

"It's not enough that I let you stay home all day while I work to pay for this house," were his first coherent words. The word "let" was an interesting one, because my keeping house was Jimmy's idea. He's one of those liberated men who have no problem with wives working, other men's wives that is. I'd been waitressing at a greasy spoon near Jimmy's law school when we met. He liked me serving him. Only him.

"God damn it, Amelia," he yelled. "You made me look bad in the front of the neighbors, letting the driveway get all slippery so I fell down. Look at my pants. They're all dirty! I'm not going to put up with this."

He pulled back his right arm, and before I knew it, his fist landed square in my stomach.

I learned then and there to be mindful of the weather. And to keep both a broom and a shovel handy.

I spent that first night trying to figure out what to do. Didn't want to go back to Mama. My step-daddy wasn't much different from Jimmy. And I couldn't afford my own place. I didn't make any money. Jimmy controlled everything. Even the house was in his name. Then, the next morning, Jimmy was real apologetic. Brought me flowers. Said it'd never happen again. And I bought it.

Guess I inherited denial from Mama.

So I went on cleaning Jimmy's house and pressing his pants. Making sure I had enough beer and chips on hand every Sunday so he and his pals could fill their guts while watching football or baseball or whatever sport was on TV. And I went on feeling my own stomach twist every time the weather turned bad.

Now you might wonder how a man can be both fastidious and a bubba. Turns out it's not that hard. Early in our marriage, Jimmy began going out most nights with the boys. Said it was for business. He'd set up his own law practice and needed to mingle. But I knew better. He loved drinking and telling lewd jokes, but he made sure he looked good doing it. Hell, when your daddy's the county judge, I guess you grow up learning the importance of looking right. That explained why he never hit my face. Wouldn't want to leave evidence for the town gossips.

I should've left him long ago. I know that now. Heck, I knew it that first snowy day. But something always held me back. I didn't have any money. Or I didn't have anywhere to go. Or I was plumb scared to be on my own. It was always some stupid reason.

Mostly, I didn't want our daughter, Charlotte, to grow up in a broken home. She loved Jimmy, and I could take the beatings. I could take 'em for her, like Mama took 'em for me to keep my step-daddy around. Besides, I couldn't blame Jimmy too much. I knew he liked things a certain way and should've tried harder to keep the house just so. By the time Charlotte grew up and moved away, the thought of leaving Jimmy was a dim memory. He was my husband, and a wife stays with her husband, for better or for worse.

Now, I don't want to give the wrong impression. We had a lot of worse, but there also was some better. Jimmy could be very sweet. He always brought home flowers on my birthday. On our anniversary we'd dress up and go out dancing. And Charlotte, well, he just doted on her. When she smiled at him, he seemed to glow from within. And to his credit, he never laid a hand on her. I would've dealt with him years ago if he had.

I guess I would've put up with Jimmy forever if he hadn't made two important changes right about the same time. First, after his daddy passed a couple summers back, Jimmy paid off our mortgage with the inheritance money, so suddenly our monthly expenses dropped way down. With the house paid off and the savings we had in the bank, I really didn't need Jimmy no more. If something happened to him, I could sell his law practice to one of his buddy competitors and make enough to be comfortable.

Second, he took up with Mandy Lee, a waitress at a diner near the main road out of town. I'm pretty sure this was Jimmy's first affair, despite that we'd been married thirty years. Frankly, I think he'd been too scared to stray till then. His daddy was real conservative and wouldn't have put up with rumors of Jimmy running around. A month had barely gone by after the old man's death before Gladys, one of the check-out gals at Food Lion, whispered to me that Jimmy'd been spotted at the Motel Six outside of town with Mandy Lee. She thought I should know. She's sweet that way.

I spent a long time trying to figure out what to do after that. I'd grown used to the beatings. But I wasn't used to being made a fool of in public. I wasn't gonna take it. Suppose I cared about my image as much as Jimmy did about his own.

So I followed Jimmy around for a week. Sly like. I wanted to be positive Gladys was right. Of course she was. Gladys always knows everything. I've always thought her talents are wasted at that supermarket. She should work for the newspaper.

Oh, how my blood boiled when I spotted Jimmy and Mandy Lee making out in the back seat of his truck, parked on a dirt road near the old lumber mill where anybody could see. Especially 'cause she must have reminded him of me, back in the day. Bleached blond hair. Lot of makeup. And a waitress, too. Not only was he cheating on me, but he'd practically chosen my twin.

What'd she see in him? Couldn't have been nothing but dollar signs. Jimmy's charm only went so far, and he hadn't quite maintained his looks. Sure he dyed his hair and exercised some, but the drink showed in his face and belly. Mandy Lee had to be after him for his money. Our money. Heck, she was twenty-five, he was fifty-five. You do the math.

No way I was gonna let that trampy waitress get her claws on my money. Trying to steal my husband was more than enough.

My first thought was divorce, of course. But given Jimmy's profession and his daddy's lingering influence, I knew Jimmy'd find a way to screw me. Besides, this is a small town, and even though I've lived here over thirty years, I'm still considered an outsider.

Didn't help that Jimmy never let me make my own friends. He liked me home by myself at his beck and call.

I could've just left him, I guess. Packed up and moved in with Charlotte on the other side of the state. Lived in the mountains instead of by the mouth of the Chesapeake Bay. But I'd spent so much time in our house, our paid-off house, I didn't want to leave it. I liked the idea that Charlotte could return to her childhood home at the holidays. That my grandbabies would have memories of the pretty ceramic figurines I sometimes bought and set on the living room mantel, much to Jimmy's wrath. I never got a good deal, he said. Always paid too much. Well, I did some calculating now, and if I took a job working retail, I could afford to keep the house. Plus it'd be nice to have a place to go to everyday instead of staying home with the TV as company. There's only so many talk shows you can watch before your brain starts to cave in.

So that left me with only one choice. I had to kill him.

Not right away mind you. Since I'd just learned of the affair—a fact Gladys would surely tell the world about—if Jimmy died then and there I'd be the prime suspect faster than gossip at a church picnic. No. I had to bide my time. Yet I couldn't wait too long, not with Mandy Lee gunning to replace me.

And I had to come up with a way to make it look like an accident. That wasn't easy. Especially since I was so angry, all I wanted to do was shove a knife in his chest and twist it round and round. Bashing his head in with a snow shovel also crossed my mind. Jimmy's beatings always got worse in the winter. Somehow I never shoveled the walk between the carport and the front door well enough for him.

I was sitting on our living room sofa a few days after I spotted Jimmy and Mandy Lee together, thinking about that snow shovel. And how Daddy died in that whiteout. That's when it came to me.

The plan was so simple it kinda scared me. The only tricky part was the timing. I had to do wait till winter and hope we got a big snow storm that started in the evening.

Now you may not approve of my plan, but I kind of think God did, 'cause he sent us that wallop of a storm last year, and early, too. It doesn't often snow a lot in Virginia, especially in December.

Little tingles pricked my arms that morning as I listened to the weather report. A nor'easter was making her way up the coast. The winds were gonna wreck havoc on the Bay, they said. Plus, they figured we'd get a good six inches at least, with the snow starting to fall late in the night. That'd be too late for my plan. But I waited all day, hoping the storm would speed up a bit.

By dinner time, the snow still hadn't started. Hopeful, I served Jimmy a meatloaf that I cooked too long. I knew that would piss him off and encourage him to go to the bar as usual, despite the impending storm. Then, during the meal, I started chattering about Oprah. Lord, he hated Oprah. That ran him out of the house fast and good.

At seven o'clock, about twenty minutes after he fled, the snow started coming. Unlike that first day he hit me, these were big flakes. Heavy ones. They fell at two inches an hour. I worried that maybe this was too much snow too quick, that God was playing an awful trick on me. If Jimmy paid attention, he might come home early to avoid the bad roads. But I didn't have another plan, and I'd made up my mind to kill him. I wouldn't spend another day being the town laughingstock.

So I got down on my knees, and I prayed. Prayed that Jimmy'd get so caught up with his good old boys that he wouldn't worry about slick roads and wouldn't start weaving up the driveway till his usual time, around eleven. I prayed he'd do the same three-point turn he'd done every night since he built that carport next to the tall bushes twenty years ago, backing in under the awning so in the morning he could hop in and take off fast. And since he'd be drunk, that fancy maneuver would take him several tries and wear him out like always, so he'd snooze in the truck before coming in the house.

I prayed to God, all the while fearing the devil would respond instead.

By nine-thirty I felt a little more confident. Enough snow had fallen, and Jimmy hadn't come home. I grabbed my trusty shovel and headed to the driveway. Over and over I scooped up piles of snow, then hauled 'em to the carport and flung 'em at the edges, until I'd created sort of an oval that Jimmy could fit his truck in. I made sure that I put more snow at the back, so there'd be a good solid mound right by the tail pipe.

Then I made a half-hearted attempt to shovel the walk to the house. I had to make it look like I had shoveled some, but I didn't need to do a good job. Not anymore. I left just enough snow on the walk to encourage Jimmy to nap in the truck, in case he thought of coming straight in. Jimmy hated walking in the snow, especially when his legs weren't that steady. And since it was so cold that night, I reckoned he'd leave the motor running and the heater on while he rested before his stagger to the front door.

I counted on it.

At a little before eleven I slid into the house. Boy, I'd cut it close. Moving all that snow took a lot more time than I'd expected. I shimmied out of my jeans and threw on a flannel nightgown. After shutting the lights, I got in bed and rolled around a bit, so it'd look like I'd been sleeping just in case he came in.

But I had no intention of sleeping.

I planned to watch.

When I heard Jimmy's truck start to rumble up our long driveway, I crept to the window. Since I'd been lying in the dark, my eyes had adjusted, and I could see pretty good outside. The moonlight reflecting off the snow helped, too.

Jimmy weaved back and forth, far more than usual. I didn't realize the driveway would be so icy. Lord, it looked like he might spin out and never make it to the carport. Then he'd leave the truck on the driveway and head on in. Boy, would he be mad then.

I held my breath for what felt like forever. Finally, thank the Lord, Jimmy made it to the carport and started his three-point-turn. The truck skidded a bit more, and I sucked in breath. Funny, even with the plan in motion, I got frightened when I thought he might be hurt. The heart's strange that way.

I almost ran out there to bring him in, but then I remembered Mandy Lee. And the pitying looks I'd been getting all over town. And I thought of all the blows I'd endured these many years. I stayed put.

The truck's tires spun as Jimmy tried to back up. He revved the engine over and over, the truck sliding this way and that. I was sure any moment he'd give up, frustrated. And then he'd come inside and share his anger with me. But just as my fear was settling into my stomach, the truck shot back. Its tail rammed right into the large mound of snow I'd created. Then Jimmy cut the lights. And like a puppet on my string, he stayed put, slumping back in the seat. That was odd, because Jimmy typically crawled in the back for his naps. I guessed he'd drank too much for his stomach to handle even that little bit of motion. Not that it mattered. His being extra drunk worked better for me.

He likely began snoring within two minutes, even before the carbon monoxide began seeping into the truck. I figured the local police would call this an accident. Hell, how was anyone down here supposed to know that snow could clog a tail pipe like that? We hardly ever get big storms.

After I watched Jimmy snooze for thirty minutes without stirring, I crept off to bed. Slept like a baby.

The sun flashed through the window the next morning, shining off all that snow outside. I threw on my heavy coat and snow boots, grabbed my shovel, and headed to the carport. Had to make finding Jimmy look authentic.

"Jimmy!" I called for the benefit of any neighbors who might be out shoveling their walks. "You old fool. What in the world were you thinking sleeping in the truck all night? You could've froze to death."

I pulled open the cab door and let out a scream. Sounded pretty authentic if I do say so myself. Jimmy was pale blue and stiff, eyes closed, his head leaning on his right shoulder. Hard to believe he'd never be able to lay a hand on me again. I ran in the house, called the ambulance. It took 'em a while make it over. The roads were pretty bad. That worked well for me, 'cause the snow had started to melt. I hoped the evidence by the tail pipe had begun to disappear too, but I didn't dare check. Didn't want to leave footprints.

Once the paramedics declared Jimmy dead, they called in the reinforcements. The cops and the medical examiner pulled up together. I stood out on the walk, arms crossed over my chest while the wind whipped through my coat. I pretended not to notice, had to look consumed by my grief.

I gave my story to the cops in between sobs that made it hard for me to breathe. (Thought that would be a nice touch.) I railed at Jimmy for going out into that storm. Was furious that he'd napped in the truck instead of coming in from the cold. If only I hadn't gone to sleep before he got home, if I'd checked on him, maybe I could've saved him.

The medical examiner ambled over from Jimmy and gave me a hard stare. "I'm sorry for your loss, Mrs. Marshall." He paused, pulling on his gray whiskers. "But your husband didn't die from the cold."

"Then what killed him, Harry?" one of the cops asked.

I looked up, trying to appear surprised.

"Well, a number of factors seemed to be at work, and I'll have to do a full autopsy to be sure, but I'd have to say it was the blow to his head that did him in."

You could've blown me over. "What blow to the head?"

"You probably didn't notice it when you pulled open the door, ma'am," the medical examiner said. "But there's a deep impression on the right side of his head. Looks like someone hit him hard."

I tried to make sense of all this but couldn't. Stunned, I went inside and called Charlotte. Pretty soon the cops took Jimmy away. And then they started asking me questions. When was the last time I saw Jimmy? Did I know anyone who'd want to hurt him? And then, with narrow eyes, they asked, how was our marriage? I'd worked so hard to make it look like an accident, and now someone else had gone off and killed Jimmy, and the cops were looking at me. Lord, maybe the devil had heard my prayers.

Eventually I must have satisfied the cops, 'cause they went off to investigate elsewhere. Probably that bar Jimmy loved so much.

For the rest of the day I sat in the house, confused as all get-out. Jimmy wasn't one to get into fights. The only person he'd ever hit was me. I couldn't make heads or tails of this turn of events. I sure was glad when Charlotte came home late that afternoon. She was a real comfort.

It may sound odd, but I felt angry that someone else had killed Jimmy. I may have wanted him dead, but he was my husband, and if anyone was gonna kill him, it shoulda been me.

I tossed and turned all night, trying to figure out who had done it. And worrying that the cops would come back to snoop over here. Would they figure out I'd tried to kill Jimmy? Would they blame me for the blow to his head?

I got my answer the next morning. The doorbell rang while I was having my second cup of coffee. I thought it was Charlotte, back quick from the florist's. I opened the door and swallowed hard. The sheriff was standing there, the handcuffs on his belt shining in the light.

"Morning, Mrs. Marshall." His voice sounded gruff from tobacco. "I'm here to talk about your husband. May I come in?"

It didn't really seem like a request. I let him in.

The sheriff walked beside me to the living room, looking at me sideways. Then he settled on the couch while I sank into Jimmy's favorite chair. He stared at me and sighed. I began feeling real jumpy and worked hard to stay still.

"My boys have done a lot of investigating in the last twenty-four hours, trying to find out how your husband ended up the way he did."

The sheriff paused and stared at me some more. A lump grew in my throat while I waited him out.

"Do you know a Mandy Lee Roulston?" he asked.

I blinked. They'd found out about the affair, and now they thought I'd struck Jimmy in revenge. And I had no alibi! I'd been home alone shoveling all that snow.

My mind raced while I tried to decide how to plead my case. "Mandy Lee. Well, um, yes, I guess I have heard that name."

The sheriff nodded, staring at the floor. "It looks like she's the one who hit your husband, ma'am. We arrested her late last night." He cleared his throat and stood. "I'm sorry I can't give you any more information right now. Just wanted you to know we'd made an arrest."

And before I could ask any questions, he'd said his good-byes and left. I stood there bug-eyed for a few minutes. They'd arrested Mandy Lee? They weren't after me? It took a bit for the news to sink in, and then I got real happy real fast. The sheriff hadn't been playing coy with me. He probably didn't feel comfortable telling me what had happened. But I knew the important stuff. Jimmy was dead. Mandy Lee'd been arrested. Jimmy would've been proud. Talk about a two-for-one deal.

A half-hour later, Gladys came by to pay a condolence call, and she had no qualms telling me what the sheriff hadn't. Thank goodness Charlotte hadn't come back, so she didn't have to hear the details right then.

Seems Mandy Lee had stopped by the bar that snowy night, and she and Jimmy had words. She was tired of waiting for him. Tired of watching me live like a queen in my nice little house while she continued to serve greasy food to men with grabby hands.

Mandy Lee told Jimmy the time had come to make a choice, and God bless Jimmy, he chose me.

Hearing that made my heart swell. Even after all these years, all the beatings and the affair, in the end he loved me. He picked me. That meant something.

Meant something to Mandy Lee, too. She chased him out of the bar, screaming her head off. Some of the boys followed to watch the show. Jimmy tried to ignore her, but at some point she belittled his manhood. Jimmy turned back and slipped in the snow.

It's hard for me to believe what Gladys said happened next, what with Jimmy caring so much about public appearances. But I guess his anger over looking like a fool clouded his senses.

He hauled off and hit Mandy Lee right in the stomach. She doubled over moaning for a moment, then ran forward, ramming her head into him. Jimmy fell back. And she started kicking him. In his stomach and his legs.

And his head.

The fight didn't last more than a minute before the bystanders broke it up. Mandy Lee stomped off, and Jimmy, humiliated, drove on home. It's a wonder he didn't run off the road. Mandy Lee had kicked him so hard, his brains had banged around his skull and started to turn to mush.

That explained why his truck swerved as he came up the driveway that night. And why he weaved so much during the three-point turn. It wasn't the snow and ice and beer after all. I kept that thought to myself.

Now that slut Mandy Lee's in prison for manslaughter, and I'm living the good life. I got a job at Becky's Hallmark Shop over in Grafton, where they sell the prettiest figurines. I get a twenty percent discount. I've finally made some friends, and I still make it home everyday in time to watch Oprah.

Turns out that years ago, Jimmy bought a heap of life insurance from one of his daddy's pals. He'd wanted to make sure his girls would be taken care of in case anything happened to him, the insurance man told me. And every year like clockwork, Jimmy upped the policy. Kind of like an inflation adjustment.

So I only have to work part time. And I have more than enough money to pay a neighbor boy to shovel the driveway whenever it snows. No way I'm gonna do it.

Yep, Jimmy's gone, but he's still taking care of me. God bless my compulsive bubba.

※

"Compulsive Bubba" first appeared in Chesapeake Crimes 3, *published by Wildside Press in 2008.*

I once saw a terrible news story about a man whose toddler died. The snow had been bad, blocking in his parked car, so he put his child in the car with the heater on while he dug the car out. He either didn't realize his car's tail pipe was snowed in, or he didn't know until it was too late that a snowed-in tail pipe could result in carbon monoxide backing up into the vehicle. That story stayed with me, and I thought I could use that tail pipe fact one day in my writing. I didn't know how, though, until Amelia, my beleaguered character in "Compulsive Bubba," started talking to me one day in the shower. Out of nowhere, I heard the story's first paragraph—in a southern accent. And then, like kismet, I recalled that tail pipe story. I rinsed off as fast as I could and ran to my computer to write Amelia's story: a southern woman using northern know-how to free herself from her abusive husband.

HAVE GUN—
WON'T TRAVEL

I had just settled into my recliner with a Coors and the remote control when I heard a gun being racked behind me.

"You feeling lucky today, Earl?"

I spilled some of my beer—damn it!—as I twisted around and ducked. My wife, Christine, was pointing a shotgun at me. And not just any shotgun. It looked like my daddy's favorite. I poked my head around the chair. Yep. It was the Mossberg 500 that Daddy used to carry when he went hunting. Its black barrel gleamed in the sunlight pouring through our living room back window, which overlooked the Allegheny Mountains.

"Now, I'm pretty sure that this old gun here isn't loaded, but I could be mistaken," Christine said, a glint in her eye and her finger nearing the trigger as she walked around to the front of my La-Z-Boy. "Think I should take a chance and fire it to be sure?"

My face grew hot as my blood pressure surely spiked. I knew that gun wasn't loaded. I checked it myself after my last hunting trip. But I still didn't like having a weapon aimed at me. Especially my own weapon.

"Let me guess," I said, sitting back up. "Jenna called again today."

Christine pointed the gun at the floor, walked to the couch, and perched on its edge. "You're darn right she called again. We didn't get two minutes into the conversation before she asked about the guns, Earl."

I slammed my beer down on the end table so hard the lamp shook. It was Friday night. I'd just put in a long week at the lumber company, and this was supposed to be my time to relax. Now I had to deal with this shit.

"They're my guns, damn it!" I said. "She has no right demanding I get rid of them."

Shaking her head, Christine set the Mossberg next to her on the couch. A lock of brown hair fell forward and hung by her cheek. "I'm not having this argument with you again. Jenna has made it clear that she won't come home to visit after the baby's born if there's a single gun here. So I want them sold." She slapped her hands against her knees. "Every last one!"

"This is what we get for letting her move away," I said. "When she wanted to go to college in D.C., what did I say?"

Christine started tapping her right foot, like she often does when I make a good point. I didn't care.

"I said no, that's what I said." I sprang up and began pacing between the recliner and the window. "I said she could get just as good an education from a state school here in West Virginia. Fairmont State's a good school. So's W.V.U. Heck, we've even got Pot State right here in Keyser. But no. You said the schools in D.C. were better. You said we should let her go. And now look what's happened. She married that liberal New Yorker and is living in hoity-toity Georgetown with all those two-faced politicians. And she's demanding that I sell my daddy's guns. Our family nest egg!"

"Nest egg?" Christine laughed. "You are just like your daddy, Earl. Convinced those guns are worth something when in reality they're probably junk."

"They're not! They're pure Americana is what they are. Heck, we've got guns from the Civil War, including one from the Battle of Droop Mountain."

Christine rolled her eyes. "Not that old yarn again."

Oh, I wanted to smack her. I'd never hit a woman, but lately Christine had been trying my patience.

"You know full well my Enfield musket was used down at Droop Mountain," I said. "And since it was the last major battle in West Virginia during the Civil War, that makes the musket valuable—not to mention it's a part of our heritage."

"It's a part of your daddy's tall-tale collection is what it is," Christine said. "No one but your daddy ever thought that gun was actually used at Droop Mountain, and you know it."

I kicked the coffee table leg so hard pain shot through my foot. "You're wrong! About that gun. About all of 'em. Daddy spent years building that collection. He knew what he was doing. Heck, that musket's probably worth a fortune."

"Prove it!" She stood up, hands on her hips. "If you think those old guns are worth something, sell 'em so we can finally afford to go on that vacation to Florida you've been promising."

I shook my head, turned to the window. I loved looking out at all those trees and the mountains behind. Why go to Florida when we've got everything we need here in Keyser? Fishing. Hunting. High school football in the fall. There's even a golf course, not that I play. Tried it once. Nearly had a stroke trying to hit that freaking ball. I took a deep breath. Our property runs five miles behind the house and a half-mile in front. Tons of privacy. What more could you want in life? Nothing. Yet Christine kept harping about taking a vacation. Stupid waste of money.

"No. This isn't the right time to sell the guns." I turned and faced her. "We need to wait till the economy picks up so we can get the best price."

Always nice when an excuse is also the truth.

Christine stared at me. "There is no more time to wait, Earl," she said, speaking slowly, as if I was a child. "Jenna's baby will be born before you know it."

I picked up my beer, took a swill, and wiped my mouth with my sleeve. "That girl has gotten entirely too big for her britches."

"There is nothing wrong with her wanting to make sure our house is safe for the baby—"

"Safe! Of course it's safe. Did we ever have any incidents with the guns while she was growing up? No. I taught her everything she needed to know about gun safety. We never keep 'em loaded. Heck, nearly every single one's an antique anyway. Probably wouldn't fire if you wanted 'em to."

"That's not the point!" Christine stepped closer, looking me square in my eyes.

"Then what the heck is the point?"

Christine breathed in and out several times, her face all red. She reminded me of those old cartoons of Toro the Bull right before he charged.

"The point, as you well know," she said, so slowly and calmly I knew she was truly reaching her limit, "is that accidents happen, and Jenna and David aren't taking any chances. All we need is one gun to have one bullet in it and for the baby to get a hold of it—"

"Ha!" I said. "I'd like to see that. A baby holding a gun."

"You know what I mean. Once the child gets old enough to run around—"

"But the guns aren't loaded!"

"Oh, you don't know that, Earl." She flopped back down on the couch, crossing her legs and waving her hand. Like she was dismissing a servant. Always made my want to wring her neck. "Most of those guns have been gathering dust in the attic for years. Your daddy used to pick 'em up anywhere, thrilled to have more firepower in the house. I bet he never checked if they were actually loaded or not, and I'm sure you didn't check every single one of them either before you put them in the cabinets."

"Well then, neither did you, if you're so concerned about safety."

"I'm not the one who's concerned. Jenna is."

"Irrationally."

"Enough!" Christine leaned forward again. "I'm sick and tired of having this argument with you. Right or wrong, those are her terms. We get rid of the guns or she won't ever come home again. So we are going to meet her terms, Earl. You hear me? You have one more month to find a dealer to come and buy all those guns."

"Or what?"

"Or what?" She narrowed her eyes and crossed her arms. "You don't want to know 'or what'."

* * * *

I leaned back in the red vinyl booth at Denny's late the next morning, sipping my black coffee. The remains of my eggs and scrapple lay on my plate. Across the table, my buddy Ted eyed me while swallowing the last of his grits. His beard was grayer than mine and had some crumbs stuck in it. We'd just returned from a few hours of trout fishing, our Saturday morning routine. Damn fool had caught a whole lot more than me today.

"So you gonna tell me what's eating you?" Ted said, pointing a strip of bacon my way. "You've been quieter than usual this morning."

Ted and I always came to Denny's after fishing. Best place for in town for breakfast and news. But I wasn't feeling my usual sociable self. I'd been replaying my argument with Christine over and over in my mind since Ted picked me up at six. I gave him the highlights.

"Well, it's not unreasonable for your girl to want you to get rid of the firearms," he said.

"Ted, you kidding me?"

He sighed. "You hear it on the news all the time. Folks think their guns are unloaded when they're not. Or kids find the ammunition and load 'em themselves. You remember what happened last year over in Cumberland."

Cumberland? "No, what happened?"

"Lord, Earl, don't you ever watch the news or read the paper? Some kid, six or seven years old, found his pappy's pistol, loaded it up, and shot his little sister in the head. He thought it was a toy."

I let out a big sigh. "Nothing good ever comes out of watching the news. That's why I only pay attention to the sports. Kids killing kids. Who wants to know about things like that?"

"People involved in the world?"

"Hmph." I tugged on my chin. When did my whiskers get so coarse? "Only time I listen to the news is if they're talking about taxes going up. And that happens all too freaking often. Damn liberal politicians. All they want is to take, take, take, right outa my pocket. And yours." I banged my fist on the table. "Anyway, something like what happened in Cumberland would never happen to me. I control what goes on in my home."

"Yeah, you and every other parent before something awful happens. Besides, it doesn't sound like you have much choice in the matter."

He was right, and that fact had been gnawing at my craw ever since Jenna brought up the damn gun issue. That's what her husband, David, called it. The "gun issue." I bet this was all his idea in the first place.

I grumbled as Rhonda came by to refill my coffee. She wasn't much to look at—graying red hair, a thick middle, and stumpy legs—but she was a great listener. She'd been waiting tables here nearly twenty years. Word was her husband had been nagging her to spend more time at home cooking for him, but she wouldn't give up this job for anything. It kept her in the loop.

"What's the matter, Earl?" Rhonda said. "Did Ted outfish you again today?"

Ted smirked.

"Or is it that fight you had with Christine last night that's making you all grumpy?" she said.

"Son of a… How do you do that, Rhonda?" I asked. "How do you know everything about everybody so damn fast?"

"Honey, this is Keyser. The gossip train's not that long. Christine talked to Lolly who told her husband, who's cousins with Bobby in the kitchen." She tilted her head toward the swinging doors behind her and raised one eyebrow.

"Of course," I said. "And now you know, so everybody knows."

Rhonda shrugged. "I don't get what all the fuss is about. If Jenna's so worked up about those guns, why don't you just put a lock on the attic door?"

My mouth fell open. Hot damn.

"Rhonda, you have earned your tip." I grinned up at her. "A lock. Why didn't I think of that before?"

* * * *

We finished eating quick so we could make it to Ace Hardware before it closed at one. Then Ted dropped me off at home. In record time I dressed the two trout I'd caught and put 'em in the fridge. Then I grabbed my toolbox from the garage and marched straight to the door leading up to the attic. I was in the middle of removing the doorknob when Christine came up behind me.

"What are you doing?" she asked.

I rose from my crouch, my knees creaking. Cripes, when did I get so old?

"I'm putting a new doorknob on so no one can get in the attic without a key." I jerked my thumb at the door. Smiled. "Solves all our problems. I don't have to sell the guns. And the baby will be safe. The only ones who'll have a key will be you and me. I knew I'd find a way to fix this mess."

Christine frowned and crossed her arms over her chest. "I don't know, Earl."

"What's not to know? It's a perfect solution."

"It's only a perfect solution if Jenna agrees. The gun cabinets are already locked, and that hasn't given her any comfort."

"Well this will. I told you. It's perfect."

"Hmm. We'll see." She turned and walked to the stairs. "Make sure you take a shower before you come back down," she called. "You smell like fish!"

* * * *

I finished explaining my solution to Jenna and David and pulled on the tangled phone cord some more so I could stretch it across the kitchen. The cord snagged on some of the utensils Christine kept in a pitcher on the counter, next to the crock pot, knife block, and can opener. Hell. Why'd she always keep so much crap out?

"Hold on, Daddy."

I heard Jenna and David talking, but they must have been covering the mouth pieces 'cause I couldn't make out what they were saying. Then, after a half minute or so: "I'm sorry, Earl, but that's not going to work," David said.

We'd called them right after dinner so they could sign off on my great idea. I couldn't believe my ears.

"Why the heck not?" I untangled the cord and began pacing across the checkered brown-and-white linoleum floor that Christine wanted to replace even though it was in perfectly good condition.

"How hard do you think it would be for a child to find your spare key, Earl?" David said. "A door with a lock on it'll draw kids like a moth to a flame. Just like those locked cabinets would. We can't risk it."

"Be reasonable, Jenna." I aimed my comment at her. She'd have the sense to override her nervous Nellie husband. "Your mother and I will keep the keys on us at all times."

The line was silent for a couple moments. I was getting to her.

"I'm sorry, Daddy," Jenna finally said, "but you can't promise me that will always be the case. It's too dangerous. David and I want the guns gone."

I gritted my teeth and growled. That girl had moved three hours east, but she might as well have moved to Mars, considering how much she'd changed. Agreeing with her high-strung husband instead of me!

"Well, you know what I want?" I held the receiver so tight my fingers ached. "I want my old Jenna back. The one who listened to me. Looked up to me. Who had the common sense God gave her."

"I'm not going to argue with you, Daddy."

"Fine," I said. "Why don't we make this real simple? You don't have to visit. Ever!" I turned and punched the wall, leaving a large dent.

Christine stormed in from the living room, where she'd been listening on the extension. She grabbed the phone and glared.

"Don't worry, honey," Christine said into the receiver. "Of course we want you and David to keep coming home. Your father's just a bit worked up. I'll take care of it." She walked to the other side of the room, trying to soothe Jenna. As if she was the one who needed soothing.

I stomped into the living room, shaking my stinging knuckles, and took a few deep breaths to keep myself from smashing that ugly end-table lamp Christine loved so much. Then I dropped into my La-Z-Boy and flipped on the TV. A pre-season football game between the Steelers and the Lions had just started. I envied the players every time they slammed into each other, letting out their aggression. Must be nice.

Christine came into the room a few minutes later, stood beside me, a large book clutched under her left arm. "I told you so, Earl."

I told you so, Earl. Whatever happened to a wife supporting her husband?

"That girl sounds more like her husband every day," I said. "No common sense at all."

Christine snorted. "There's someone in this family lacking common sense, but it's not Jenna."

I snorted back. "What's that you're holding?"

She tossed the book to me. The yellow pages.

"What's this for?"

"There must be a section on gun dealers in there, Earl. Use it. And make sure you fix that drywall!"

* * * *

A couple hours later, Christine had gone up to bed with one of her women's magazines. I was polishing off my third beer. The Lions were ahead. Unbelievable.

I'd gone through that phone book several times. Found lots of ads from folks willing to take my guns off my hands. Collectors. Pawn brokers. Antique shops. Gun shops. Rip-off artists. Every single one of 'em.

I dropped the book on the floor with a thud. No way to tell which of these guys would be trustworthy. Or if any of them would be. I thought about checking the Internet for collectors, but I'd face the same problem there. I even considered reaching out to Stan from work—he has a cousin who collects. But you can't even count on getting a good deal from folks you know, and I couldn't stand the thought of being swindled. Daddy had spent so long building his collection. Remington revolvers. Ballard carbines. He had guns from every American war going back to the Civil War, including the Enfield musket and a Gatling gun. I couldn't sell them to just anyone. I thought for a second about moving the guns to a storage unit, but the chances of being robbed were far too great. No way I'd risk that.

I sighed and took another pull on my beer. I'd think about it tomorrow when my head was clearer.

* * * *

A few weeks went by. I hadn't been able to figure out who I could trust. So I'd done nothing. To avoid Christine's nagging, I began putting in longer hours at the lumber company and spending my evenings at Clancy's pub in town. After a while, Christine stopped asking me if I'd found a buyer for the guns. In fact, she started avoiding me, too, disappearing into the cellar for hours doing God knows what. Not that I cared. I'd worn her down, won the argument. Jenna would come around, too, eventually. She'd have to.

Ted picked me up for our usual Saturday morning fishing trip. The air had a nip to it, and the leaves had begun to turn. Bright oranges, reds, and yellows. They reflected off the water as the sun peeked in and out behind the clouds. Even the trout loved the weather. They kept coming up to the surface. Ted and I made a haul.

We were in a deep discussion about the Steelers's chances for the Super Bowl this year when we walked into Denny's. Rhonda showed us to a booth, took our orders, and said she'd bring our coffees right out.

"Hey, there's a guy with taste as bad as yours." Ted laughed, looking past me.

I turned around and spotted a guy I recognized from church— Christine attends every Sunday, I go less often—sitting near the door. He was wearing a dark red and green plaid jacket. Looked like he was about to polish off some sausage.

I laughed, too, twisting back. "That's a great jacket. Looks just like mine. It woulda come in handy this morning before it warmed up."

"Why don't you wear that ugly thing anymore?" Ted asked.

I sighed. "Christine hates it. And I got this coffee stain on the collar she couldn't get out. That's how I ended up getting that new black coat a couple years ago."

"Oh, yeah," Ted said, nodding.

"I should drag out that plaid jacket for old times' sake. It would drive Christine nuts."

"Don't you have enough problems these days without trying to piss her off?"

"It's my jacket, Ted. I should be able to wear what I want. I've been letting Christine push me around too much lately."

Rhonda came by with our coffees and, a couple minutes later, our food. As I dug into my eggs over easy, I told her how well Ted and I had done that morning at the pond.

"Boy, Earl, you're sure in a good mood, considering," she said.

"Of course I'm in a good mood. You shoulda been there, Rhonda. The air was crisp. The sky a deep blue. You could see for miles. The shadow of the Alleghenies made it a picture-perfect scene. And the fish. Oh, the fish were practically begging us to catch 'em. I swear one of them jumped out of the water, right onto my hook. Smiled at me."

She laughed. "If you say so, Earl."

Rhonda walked away, pouring more coffee for other customers before pushing through the swinging doors into the kitchen.

"What'd she mean by that?" Ted asked.

"What'd she mean by what?" I slid some hash browns on my fork. God, I loved hash browns.

"She said that you're certainly in a good mood, considering. Considering what?"

Huh. "I don't know." I swallowed the hash browns and glanced toward the kitchen. Rhonda still hadn't come out. "It's probably nothing. You know how she likes to talk."

I caught Ted rolling his eyes. What was that about?

"Anyway," I said. "Getting back to the Steelers." We talked about their draft picks, and Ted invited me to watch tomorrow's game at his house. He had one of them big-screen TVs. I'd buy one if I could only afford it.

Rhonda came around with coffee refills. "What do you think of the Steelers's chances this year?" I asked her.

"They'll be lucky if the Ravens don't stomp them back into the twentieth century," she said. "Your running back's got a case of the fumbles lately."

"You wish." I shook my head. "Besides, the Steelers's defense is tops, bar none. Ain't that right, Ted?"

He nodded, sipping his coffee. Coward. Ted never got involved when I baited Rhonda.

"Rhonda, your Baltimore boys are going down this year," I said.

She shook her head. "You pick this same fight with me every fall, Earl. Give it up. The Steelers suck, and you know it."

"Rhonda, Rhonda, Rhonda." I let out a big sigh. "There goes your tip."

"Big loss."

She winked at me and had just turned toward the next booth when I remembered Ted's question. "Hey, Rhonda, what'd you mean before when you talked about my mood?"

"What?" She stepped back.

"You said I'm in a good mood, considering. Considering what?"

"Oh," she said. "Considering the yard sale."

"Yard sale?"

She looked at me like I'm crazy. "Yeah, the one going on at your house as we speak."

I laughed. "Rhonda, for once, you have got your gossip all wrong. There is no yard sale going on at my house."

She set her coffee pot down on our table, stepped over to the counter, and grabbed a copy of the *News-Tribune* lying there. She returned, flipping pages, and handed me the paper open to a page full of classified ads. Dogs for sale. Garage sales. Help-wanted ads.

"So?" I said.

She sighed and pointed her stubby finger at an ad near the bottom of the first column.

Yard Sale. 2902 Pine Road. Sat. 9/18. Starts 8 a.m. Household items, clothing & more.

I'd be damned. Rhonda was right. Why didn't Christine tell me?

"The ad's been running for the last few days," Rhonda said. "I hear Christine's trying to get rid of a lot of your old junk. Plus all your guns."

"My guns!" Heads turned my way, but I didn't care. "C'mon, Ted, I've gotta get home."

I threw some cash on the table and hustled toward the door, Ted right behind me.

"Son of a bitch," I said as we rushed past the guy from church. "That is my jacket!"

* * * *

The tires on Ted's pickup squealed as we turned onto Swamp Road, a couple miles from my house.

"I can't believe it. I can't fucking believe it."

I'd been saying that over and over since we peeled out of the Denny's lot. How could Christine do this? She doesn't know anything about guns. How's she going to know if she's getting a good price? Son of a bitch!

"Ted, can't you go any faster?"

"Faster?" He looked at me wide-eyed. "On this road? I've just missed a deer, raccoon, and God knows how many squirrels. Just calm yourself down. We'll be there in a few minutes."

This was one of those times I wished I had one of them cell phones I see everyone else carrying. I'd refused to get one on principle. Wouldn't let Christine have one either. Didn't see a good reason to pay extra money when we have perfectly good phones right at home.

"Look!" I pointed as we slowed at a stop sign. A couple yard-sale posters were stapled to it, including a big one for my house. "Damn it all to hell. Now everyone driving through the neighborhood will know about it." I pounded my fist against the dashboard as bile churned in my stomach.

"Hey, watch it!" Ted said.

He hit the gas again. One more mile to go.

"You think it's too late?" I asked. "Someone could be buying my guns at this very moment. The sale's been going on for hours."

"You'll find out soon enough."

I ran my hand through my hair. If only I hadn't spent so much time trash-talking with Rhonda, I'd be home by now.

The next couple minutes felt like hours as we zoomed toward my place. Finally we turned onto my long driveway. Several cars were parked alongside it. And then the house came into view.

"Blast it," I said. "Look at all those people."

I recognized friends and neighbors mixed among a bunch of strangers. All of them picking through my stuff. But not the guns. I didn't see them set out anywhere. Christine was sitting in a lawn chair with a strongbox in her lap. She looked pleased as punch.

Ted hit the brakes, and I jumped from the pickup before he'd come to a full stop. Christine saw me and rose, a smile on her face, the same glint in her eye she'd had the day she pulled the gun on me.

"Surprise!" she said walking across the lawn.

"Tell me you didn't sell 'em!"

"Sell what?"

Boy, could she play coy when she wanted to. I grabbed her arm and yanked her to me. "The guns! My daddy's guns."

People turned and stared. Damn busybodies.

"Lower your voice." Christine pulled away. She rubbed her arm as she headed to our front door. "And yes, they're all gone. I sold two on Thursday—"

"Thursday!"

"And then early this morning, a guy came and bought all the ones I had left."

Gone. They were all gone. Even the Enfield musket, our own piece of state history. Gone. I tried to swallow, but my throat had this big lump in it.

"How could you do this to me?"

"Don't you blame me. You did this to yourself. You had months to sell the guns, but you refused to do it."

"Excuse me," a white-haired lady interrupted. "How much do you want for this radio?"

"Ten dollars," Christine said.

"I'll give you five."

"Sold."

The lady handed over the money and walked away with the radio that I used to listen to in the summers when I grilled on the deck. Back when Jenna lived with us. Before she changed and started all this.

Christine turned. "I told you if you didn't get rid of those guns, I'd take matters into my own hands. Well, I have."

"Did you sell 'em just like that?" I asked. "Taking whatever the buyer offered you? Heck, how much did we get ripped off today, Christine?"

"If you were so concerned about getting the best price, you should have taken care of this yourself. You could have had them appraised. Approached dealers. Antique markets. But you decided to sit on your ass and do nothing. You thought that I'd let you drive our daughter away. Well you were wrong." She took a deep breath. "I wasn't willing to put in all that effort if you weren't, but I did do a little research before today, Earl. We got a good price."

"A good price, huh? Well, what'd we get?"

She inched closer. "We made $10,000 total on all the guns."

I sputtered, and my right eye began to twitch. "That's it? Those guns were worth a whole lot more than that!"

"No they weren't. I got that information straight from Harvey Bentler."

"Who?"

"You know. From church. Always sits in the third pew on the end."

Like I pay that much attention.

She sighed at my obvious ignorance. "Tall, thin. About eighty-five years old. Walks a little stooped over."

"Oh. That guy. What's he got to do with this?"

"He's retired now, but he used to be a gun dealer. He still collects. He's a nice man. I knew I could trust him, him being a churchgoer and all, so I invited him over for tea on Thursday and asked him what he thought of your collection."

"And?"

"He said most of it wasn't worth much."

Fool woman, listening to some stranger instead of me. "Of course he did."

She crossed her arms, clutching the cashbox to her chest. "They weren't in good condition, Earl. They were rusty, he said. Flawed. Except for one of your rifles—he called it a 'beauty' and offered me $6,000 for it. He also liked that Enfield musket, despite the termite damage. Said it was probably worth $800 tops, but he offered me a $1,000 because of the Droop Mountain story, even though he didn't believe it."

"Did you take the money?"

"Yes. I knew Harvey would give me a fair price on both weapons. I took the check to the bank straight away."

"A check?" I kicked at the grass. "You handed over the guns and took a check? You're way too trusting. That check's probably gonna bounce from here to Ohio."

Her eyebrows arched up. "Shame on you, Earl. Harvey is a member of our church. That check won't bounce."

"And the rest of the guns?" I asked.

"He wouldn't buy them. Said the whole lot was worth maybe $3,000. He pointed out one we might get $500 for, another $300, but most of them were worth about $100 or less, he said. So when a guy came by early this morning and offered me $2,500 for all of them, I bargained with him. We got the $3,000 Harvey recommended. In cash." She tapped on the strongbox in her arms. "Which brings us to a grand total of $10,000 for all your guns. A good price. And you didn't have to lift a finger."

Was she right about the money? I'd always thought we had a gold mine in our attic. The Enfield itself was a real antique. It had to be worth more than $1,000. And I bet that "beauty" old Harvey bought was worth a lot more than $6,000. If I had to lose the collection, all the history, I at least should've been paid what they're worth.

I squeezed my hands into fists. I needed to hit something. Hard.

"Don't look so glum, Earl. It had to be done. And besides, now we can use some of this money to buy that big-screen TV you've been wanting."

Big-screen TV?

"We can go shopping as soon as the yard sale's over," she said. "And after we buy your TV, I'm booking our tickets. Florida, here we come."

* * * *

Ted came over the next afternoon to help me carry in my new TV and install it. It's a monster sixty-four-incher. Then he stuck around for the game. I couldn't believe how great the Steelers looked. I felt like I was right there, eating the hot dogs, smelling the sweat. A damned shame they were losing.

I tried not to think about the guns, but every time a commercial came on they swam right into my mind. Daddy's legacy was gone, just like that. And all we had to show for it were ten thousand measly dollars. Christine had no right to sell those guns. They were mine! Selling 'em was my choice to make, damn it!

When the game ended, Ted headed home, and I sat brooding in my recliner, waiting on dinner. Christine should've timed it better. Wasn't the lasagna finished baking yet? I was hungry. First my guns were sold out from under me, then the Steelers lost, and now I couldn't even have dinner when I was starving.

The news came on, and I popped open another Coors. Maybe they'd show the few good plays we'd had in the sports re-cap. Boy, I never noticed how large that announcer's nose was before.

"And coming up," she said, "we'll have an interview with a man who purchased a gun worth a reported quarter of a million dollars at a yard sale yesterday in Keyser, West Virginia."

My eye began twitching again, and I gulped down air. I knew it! I knew Daddy's collection was valuable. Oh, my fucking Lord!

I threw my beer against the wall, jumped up, and stomped to the window. A quarter of a million dollars. Lost! No, not lost. Given away. Like it was nothing.

Shaking, I stormed back across the room, picked up that ugly lamp Christine loved, and smashed it.

She ran out of the kitchen. "What's going on?"

I spun around. "You did this."

"Did what?"

I strode toward her. I'd worked hard my whole life waiting for my payoff, and she just gave it away.

"You bitch!" I spat out the words. "You fucking bitch."

Christine's eyes grew wide. I'd never talked to her like that before. All my life, I'd treated her with respect, and look where it landed me. No more!

She backed into the kitchen. "Earl, you're scaring me. What's going on?"

I laughed. "What's going on? One of those guns you gave away for practically nothing yesterday is worth a quarter of a million dollars. That's what's going on."

"What?"

"It's on the God damn news!"

I grabbed a plate off the kitchen table and threw it against the wall. It shattered. Christine screamed. I shoved her against the wall, grasped her throat, and squeezed.

Tears sprang from her eyes as she struggled, gasping and turning purple. Then she kneed me in the crotch. My grip loosened. She squirmed away. Ran into the living room. Wincing, I stumbled for a second, spotted the knife block on the counter, grabbed a large blade, and chased her.

I caught up with her at the front door. She never made it outside.

I stood there a few minutes. Panting. Staring at her lying there. Her face pale. A pool of blood seeping into the beige carpeting. Then the phone rang. I noticed the bloody knife in my hand and dropped it. Backed up.

What had I done?

"And for our final story," the newscaster said, "we have a man who bought a gun worth a reported quarter of a million dollars at a yard sale yesterday in Keyser, West Virginia. Reporting from Keyser is our correspondent Page Schelts."

I looked up while the phone kept ringing.

"Thank you, Nina. I'm here today with Randy Hix, who's had the biggest surprise of his life."

I didn't recognize the guy. Short. Thin. Squirrely looking. He was standing on a road with the reporter, a big tree behind them.

"Yeah, I like collecting guns," the guy said. "Ya never know what you're gonna get, especially at a yard sale. I bought a few yesterday. When I fully inspected this one gun after I got home, I had a feeling it was worth a whole lot more than I paid, so I went and had it appraised right away. And lo and behold, it's worth a quarter of a million smackeroos."

Smackeroos. Oh, I'd smack the huge smile off that guy's face. Finally the damned ringing stopped, and our answering machine kicked in.

"And you bought the gun, a Colt Walker, here at a house on Pine Road in Keyser," the reporter said, turning to the camera as it panned out. "The prior owner didn't want to discuss the matter on camera after we informed him of the gun's value."

I swallowed hard as I stared at the house that came on screen—a neighbor's home down the street.

Jesus Christ. I'd killed her for nothing! Now I won't have Christine. And I won't have Keyser. They'll send me to prison with no fishing or hunting or foot—

"Mama, Daddy, you there?" Jenna's voice filled the room, tinny from the answering machine. "Oh well. I wanted to tell you that I felt real bad about being so hard-nosed about the guns, Daddy. I know how much they mean to you, and I decided putting a couple locks on the attic door would work, as long as we're all vigilant. We'll have to make sure the gun cabinets are locked up tight, too. Took me a bit of doing, but I've convinced David. So you can relax, Daddy. Everything's going to be just fine. Hope you both have a wonderful night."

I fell back into my La-Z-Boy with my mouth hung open. If I'd had even one gun left, I'd have shoved it in and pulled the trigger.

❧

I thought a lot about whether to include this story in this collection. I feared that people would think I'm trying to make a statement about gun control. While I have strong views on the subject of guns (which I'm not revealing here), let me make plain that my agenda with "Have Gun—Won't Travel" was nothing more than telling a good story. The idea for this story was sparked by a newspaper article about a man who spent $45 on photograph negatives (and other things) at a garage sale and later learned the negatives might have been from photographs taken by Ansel Adams, and possibly worth $200 million. That story got me thinking about what else could be sold at a garage sale, and this tale developed from there.

I offer my thanks to author Christina Freeburn for providing me telling details about her home of Keyser, West Virginia, where this story is set. Once I decided I wanted to have guns sold at a yard sale, I had to find a location where that could happen. And under West Virginia law, it's possible (under certain conditions).

AN OFFICER AND A
GENTLEMAN'S AGREEMENT

West Point, New York. 1972.

"Holy mother of God! What have you done?"

I finished off the exclamation point at the end of "Beat Navy!," which I'd just spray painted on the grass near where the bonfire would soon be lit. Next to the goat. It was warm for early December, but I could still see my breath in the moonlight as I turned and smiled at my roommate, Pete.

"Pretty cool, huh?" We were going to go down in cadet history as having pulled off the best prank ever!

Pete's mouth hung open as he tried to form some words. What was his problem?

"How could you have done this?" Pete finally said. "You killed him. You killed Bill the Goat!"

I glanced down at the Navy mascot. His white coat, the grass beneath him, and the big N on the jacket the squids made him wear were stained red. The metallic smell of blood invaded my nose.

An hour ago I'd driven to the abandoned barn where Pete and I'd stashed the goat, alive, early this morning after driving all night back from Maryland. I painted its horns Army black and gold, then wrestled it again into the back of Pete's station wagon to bring it to campus. It had been no small task sneaking that goat past the sentry. Killing it at the barn would have been a lot easier, but I hadn't wanted to get blood all over Pete's car.

"So? What are you so upset about?" I slipped the paint can into my coat pocket, pulled out Pete's car keys, and tossed them to him. "It's just a stupid animal. Besides it crapped all over the back of your car last night. You should be thrilled."

Pete stared at me. "Thrilled? What the hell is wrong with you, Jack? The plan was to bring Bill back here, paint his horns, show him off, get a little glory before tomorrow's Army-Navy game, and then return him. Alive!"

"Don't get your panties in a twist. It's not like old Bill here hasn't been goat-napped before. Where's the glory in that? Now this"—I pointed a thumb at the carcass—"this will bring us fame beyond your imagination."

"Fame? More like infamy." Pete paced back and forth for a few moments, shaking his head. "It's one thing to kill an animal for food, but to slit its throat for…for what? Fun? You think this is fun?"

"Yeah, I do. I never realized you were such a wuss, Pete."

I surveyed my work. "Beat Navy!" in big gold letters. Right underneath: the stinking Navy goat. This was the coolest thing any cadet at West Point had ever done. How could Pete not get that?

I heard voices approaching and grabbed Pete's arm. "Come on." I yanked him behind some big bushes. "You can see for yourself how great everyone else is gonna think this is."

A couple of cadets came from the direction of the mess hall. Probably plebes. I didn't recognize them.

"Holy crap!" the one with the orange hair said as they spotted the goat and rushed over. "It's the Navy mascot."

I nudged Pete and mouthed the word, "See?"

"I'm going to be sick," the other plebe said as they bent over the goat. "Is this someone's idea of a joke?"

"No one I know," Carrot Top said. "You'd have to pretty warped to murder a goat."

"We better tell someone," the other plebe said. "I hope they catch whoever did this and shoot him. Psychotic bastard."

"Shoot him and then expel him," Carrot Top said as they ran off.

I swallowed hard. Psychotic? Warped? How did they not get how great this was? A prank worthy of the best college in the country. In the world. I should be adored for this, not reviled.

Pete stood and started walking away, his hands stuffed in his pockets.

"Hey, where are you going?"

He turned to me, his eyes hard and cold. "I'm going to the commandant. I'm going to tell him how we kidnapped Bill. I'm going to tell him everything."

I sprang up and blocked his way. "Oh no, you're not. Go cry in your girlie journal if you want, but keep your mouth shut. You're not going to let your guilty conscience ruin my life."

"You may not care about the honor code, Jack, but I do. Out of my way."

"No. Look, I thought this would be funny. A joke. How was I to know that no one would get it?" He tried to push past me. "You can't say anything, Pete. You can't do that to me."

"It's all about you, huh, Jack?"

I saw my future slipping away and thought fast. "No, it's about you, too. You spill your guts, and I'll do the same. I'll tell them how it was all your idea to go to Maryland. How we took your car. How you goaded me into it. Held the goat down while you had me do your dirty work."

"You lying son of a—"

"They'll believe me, Pete, once they see how distraught I am. Just you watch. Besides, I'm near the top of our class. I'll get away with a slap on the wrist, and in the spring, I'll get my commission. But you, old buddy, you'll be silenced and expelled. Your life destroyed. How do you think your pop the colonel will feel about that?"

I held my breath. Would he buy it?

His face paled as the wind coming off the Hudson River picked up. He bought it. Now to close the deal.

"Look, neither of us has to pay for this…mistake," I said. "You go clean out the wagon. I'll wash my hands and pitch my shirt and the spray paint where no one will find them. And we'll both keep our mouths shut. No one ever has to know."

"I'll know." Pete chewed on his lower lip so long, I thought I'd lost him. But then he nodded his agreement. "Don't ever speak to me again," he said as he turned away. "Our friendship is over."

I rolled my eyes. Like that was a big loss.

* * * *

Great Falls, Virginia. 2010.

As I stepped into the kitchen from the garage, the mingled scents of lemon and garlic made my stomach grumble. I scanned the Tuscan-style furnishings. No pots on the stove. No plates on the table. I knew I smelled food. Where the heck was Sandra? And more important, where was dinner?

The sound of the glass door off the deck sliding open answered my first question.

"Jack, there you are," Sandra said, coming inside.

She looked just right in that yellow dress I like—the one that made other men eat their hearts out. Their wives might be old and dried up, but simply the sight of Sandra still excited me. You'd never know she just turned fifty.

"I was afraid you forgot about dinner," she said.

"Dinner?"

She gave me her exasperated look, eyebrows shot to the sky, head tilted to the right. "Yes, dinner with my friend Deb and her husband. I reminded you this morning."

Christ. The book club friend. She'd been pleasant enough the couple times I'd met her, but to have to eat dinner with her and her husband? I just put in a long day at the Pentagon, and now I had to spend the evening being polite and friendly.

Sandra pulled a glass bowl from the fridge. Looked like gazpacho. "C'mon. I've set out some bread and tapenade, and we have a nice bottle of Pinot open."

I suppressed a sigh and stepped outside, glad for the privacy the battalion of trees in our backyard provided, despite the leaves that sometimes dropped into the pool. At least I didn't always have to smile at annoying neighbors.

As Sandra began introductions, Deb—even pudgier than I remembered—stood. A scarecrow of a guy rose beside her. "Jack, you remember Deb. I'd like you to meet her husband, Peter."

No way. No freaking way. His hair was gray and receding, and lines marred his face, but he otherwise hadn't changed much. I grinned and said hello to the wife, then stuck my hand out at Pete. "You old goat."

He smiled tightly—the kind of expression subordinates have after I've chewed them out and they have to take it. "Jack." He shook my hand fast and hard. "It's been a long time."

"You two know each other?" Sandra said. "That's wonderful. From where?"

"Back at the Academy." I settled into my favorite deck chair as Sandra handed me a goblet of wine. A hint of citrus wafted from it. "Pete and I were in the same class."

"What a small world," Sandra said as she eased into her usual chair. "Deb, did you know about these two?"

Deb shook her head, eyeing her husband. "No. Peter didn't mention it when he suggested this dinner. But then he never talks about those days. In fact, he doesn't like to talk about his time in the Army at all."

"Yeah, I heard you washed out after Nam," I said. "How'd your old man feel about that?"

Sandra shot me a look, but I wanted to see how far I could push Pete.

His fists clenched. "I read about your nomination in the *Post* last week, Jack." Pete's voice was steady, but I'd scored a direct hit. "Chairman of the Joint Chiefs of Staff. Quite an accomplishment."

I let a big smile cross my face. "It's nice when the president appreciates your work."

"I bet it is." Pete downed some of his wine. "Whoever would've thought you'd get so far in your career?"

"Jack's going to be a four-star general." Sandra beamed.

Deb offered congratulations while Pete chewed his lower lip. He was jealous! I nearly laughed.

"Big job," Pete said. "You'll be chief military adviser to the president?"

You bet your ass I will. "That's right."

"The Senate has to approve your nomination?" Pete asked.

"Yep."

For a split second, I could've swore I saw a gleam in Pete's eyes.

"Hmm," he said. "Hope that goes okay."

* * * *

The following Tuesday at fifteen hundred hours I stepped into the darkness of the Old Brogue Irish Pub, a few miles from my house. The place reeked of fried food. Pete had suggested it yesterday on the phone. Said it shouldn't be crowded. We could talk. I wasn't sure what he wanted to talk about, but I figured I'd hear him out.

I ordered a Guinness at the bar and spotted Pete. He wasn't hard to find. There were only three people in there, besides the bartender. Pete had parked himself with his back to the wall at a table in the far corner. The other two patrons sat at the bar—two old guys arguing about the Washington Nationals as the game blared on an overhead TV.

I set my beer on Pete's sticky table and sat. "Charming place."

"It'll do." He leaned forward. "I've spent most of the past week thinking about you, Jack. You said you heard I...how'd you so delicately phrase it? Oh yeah, 'washed out after Nam.'"

I smirked.

"Well, you should know that I've kept some tabs on you, too," Pete said. "I may not have stayed in the Army, but I have plenty of friends who did. And I've heard the rumors."

"Rumors?"

"The whispers about you. About the chances you've taken. The lives you've risked. And lost."

"Aah." I waved my hand at him. If he were a gnat, I'd have swatted him away. "Is this what you wanted to talk about? Lies made up by jealous personnel?"

"I heard about Desert Storm. You got promoted on the backs of innocent civilians. Dead civilians. Women. Children."

My face began feeling hot. Who was this turd to talk about me?

"And then Afghanistan. You managed to deflect blame in that friendly-fire incident, but folks still know what you did."

"You don't know what you're talking about." It took all my strength to keep my voice low, when I really wanted to push the table aside and punch his face in.

"I know you're the same guy you were at the Academy. I could tell that from one evening at your house. You make excuses. You'll do anything for glory. You don't care who you hurt or who you have to scare or threaten to keep your secrets."

"You better watch yourself, Pete."

He lifted a manila folder off the wooden chair beside him, opened it up, and scattered a slew of papers on the table. Copies of newspaper articles about that damn goat. Some from 1972, but others from throughout that decade, and the '80s, the '90s. Even one dated last year. Jesus.

"You're dragging out this old tale," I said. "Who cares? You think you can scare me with this?"

He stubbed his finger at the most-recent article. "They've never given up trying to figure out who killed Billy. It's been a black eye on the Academy all these years. And it's been the memory that's rotted my gut. I didn't wash out after Nam. I left. I couldn't bear to lead a platoon anymore, not when I didn't truly have honor. You stole that from me, Jack."

"Stole it?" I laughed. "Either you have honor, Pete, or you don't. Don't blame your failings on me."

He sipped his beer and sat quietly for a moment. "You're right," he said. "My biggest mistake was letting you use my father against me. My fear of disappointing him. So I kept my mouth shut, broke the code, and lost my honor. And that's on me."

What a pansy.

He leaned in again. "But you murdered the Navy mascot. And that, Jack, is on you. You think the Senate will confirm your nomination if they learn what you did? Not in this day and age, old pal."

"Dream on. You have no proof."

He laughed. "I don't need proof. The allegations would be enough to do you in. So do yourself a favor. Withdraw your nomination and retire. Save your wife the embarrassment of learning who you really are." He stood and threw down a ten-dollar bill. It landed on top of the articles. "You can keep those. I have my own copies. You've got forty-eight hours, Jack. Do the right thing, or I'll spill my guts."

Pete brushed past me. I leapt up, grabbed his arm, and bent toward his ear. "You talk about honor. Well, we had an agreement all those years ago to keep our little prank between ourselves. You want to have honor? Honor that."

He shook my hand away. "That's the difference between us, Jack. You still think it was a harmless prank. I let you build your career on that dead goat. I let a man capable of that atrocity go on to rise through the ranks of our military. There's no honor in that."

Seething, I watched him walk away. When he neared the door, I followed him out. Watched him get in his silver Lexus. Memorized his license plate.

Who had forty-eight hours, Pete?

* * * *

Four weeks later, I strode through a Senate hallway in my full dress uniform, my rack of fruit salad prominent on my chest. I'd earned every one of those medals and ribbons, and I wanted the whole world to see them.

The Committee on Armed Services had begun its hearing on my nomination early this morning, and things were proceeding just fine. As they should. No tough questions. No scandal like Pete had threatened. The senators had treated me with the respect I deserved. My future—and legacy—were secured.

It was too bad about Pete. But he'd brought it on himself. That terrible accident.

The post-lunch hallway was crowded. I shook a few hands and slapped some backs as I approached the hearing room. The afternoon session would begin in a couple minutes. I headed toward my seat.

As I strode up the aisle, I slowed. Who was that sitting at the other witness table? It looked like… No, it couldn't be.

I walked closer. Deb?

I hadn't seen her since the funeral. Sandra said she hadn't been doing well. That she'd been holed up in her house, going through Pete's things. Practically clinging to them. What was she doing here? Now?

She reached out for the pitcher of water on the table. I spotted a manila folder open in front of her. Jesus, those damn goat articles! My heart sped up. That dumb bitch was going to try to ruin me.

I forced myself to take some deep breaths. I'd faced tougher adversaries before. I'd just discredit her. She didn't know anything. She had no proof.

"If you'll all take your seats," the committee chairman announced, "we're about to reconvene."

I glared at Deb while I pulled back my chair, and I noticed a few books laid out before her. Books with blank gold covers. They looked so familiar, but from where?

The chairman called the hearing to order, and as I settled into my seat, my memory clicked: Pete's sissy journals from West Point. The ones I'd made fun of. The ones he'd written in every day about his dreams and his failures.

And all his secrets.

※

"An Officer and a Gentleman's Agreement" first appeared in Murder to Mil-Spec, *published by Wolfmont Press in 2010.*

I wrote this tale for a charity anthology to be filled with stories involving veterans or active-duty military personnel. I didn't want to write a story involving battle because I had no experience to draw from and didn't want to get the details wrong. But I wanted to take on this challenge, so I figured I'd write about U.S.-based personnel. I came up with the story's title first, which almost never happens for me, and then I batted some plot ideas around with a now-former boss. He suggested writing something involving the Navy mascot, and the story evolved from there. I worried that a story involving the death of an animal might turn off some readers, but I hoped they (and you, dear reader) would accept it if the death happened off page and there was justice for the animal in the end.

This story required a bit more research than most of my other stories, and I have certain people to thank: Andy Wachtel, for suggesting I tap into the Army/Navy rivalry; author Vincent O'Neil, an Army veteran, who helped me with details about West Point (despite his misgivings about what I planned to write—any mistakes are my own); the employees in the goat barn at Frying Pan Farm Park in Herndon, Virginia, for providing helpful information about goats; and actor Jack Nicholson, who I don't know, but whose portrayal of Col. Nathan "You Can't Handle The Truth" Jessup in A Few Good Men *inspired me and helped me find the voice for my character Jack (yes, named after him).*

EVIL LITTLE GIRL

July 1977

Pushing my bangs off my forehead, I slapped away the water droplet inching its way toward my nose, glad to take my anger out on something.

Since we'd left the pool a couple minutes ago, my bunkmates had been singing that song again. That same obnoxious song they'd sung over and over since we'd arrived at camp a week ago. The song that made me want to claw their eyes out.

"Short People."

They sang loudly, and they sang off key, and over and over, they turned to me, laughing.

I so wanted to make a snide comment back at them. Something to cut them down to size. But I knew better. Every time I'd ever stood up for myself, it had only made things worse. So I clutched my towel closer, put my head down, and tried to ignore them. It wasn't easy since we were all going to the same place. The "tween" cabin at Camp Quinnehtukqut, where—my parents had assured me—I'd make great friends. Friends for life, Mom had said.

She always said stuff like that, even though she'd never introduced me to any friends she'd known since she was twelve.

Back at the cabin, I headed to the showers in the rear of the building, and the usual snickering began. My so-called friends had all begun blossoming, as my grandma would sickeningly say. I remained flat. Flat and short. So much shorter than all the other girls my age that when I'd gotten off the bus a week ago, one of the counselors had mistakenly sent me to the nine-year-olds' cabin. Completely humiliating. When I finally found the right cabin, I held my breath as I climbed the porch stairs. Maybe this place wouldn't be like home. Maybe I would make friends here. Good friends. Those lifer friends Mom always talked about.

Instead I walked in and met Darla.

"Hey! Who let the baby in here?" She smirked, then started sucking her thumb. The other four girls mimicked her, then laughed at me. Our counselor, Gina, was nowhere to be seen. Nice introduction to sleep-away camp.

I tried all week to laugh off things like that and be friendly, the way Dad always encouraged. But it didn't help. I wasn't into boys, so I didn't know what to say when Darla and the others panted over Shaun Cassidy and the Hardy Boys TV show. My hair wasn't long enough to feather, so I couldn't bond with the girls over hairspray and Farrah Fawcett. And of course I was a head shorter than them. My size seemed to bring out their venom.

Mom always said being petite was a good thing, but I knew the truth. It sucked. It sucked so much that sometimes it took all my strength not to start smashing things.

That night at dinner, Darla loosened the lid on a saltshaker, then knocked it all over me and my food, to howls from the rest of the girls. It was a small thing, but I'd had enough. I had to get out of there, away from Darla and her friends, who thought it was cool to be called brats. I had to go home.

But Mom and Dad would never let me leave camp early. Dad would call this summer a character-building experience. Keep trying and toughen up, he'd say. Mom would tell me to smile more and give the girls another chance. They never got it when I complained about the girls at school, and they wouldn't get it now. I had to find a reason for them to come take me home. A reason even they couldn't ignore.

Maybe I could get hurt. Break my arm. No, I didn't want to do that. Maybe I could break Darla's arm. Mighty tempting, but I didn't want to get in trouble. I just wanted to go home.

I scanned the large dining hall and spotted Jason Bartlett laughing with his friends on the other side of the room, while the older girls nearby gazed on dreamily. Bingo. Jason was sixteen. Tan with wavy brown hair. Very popular. He had just been named captain of the camp tennis team. I, of course, had never talked to him.

It didn't matter. As soon as the meal ended and our free-play time began, I ran to the porch of the camp office so I'd be first in line to use the pay phone. I called home collect, like I had twice that week already. Thankfully Mom answered.

"Hi, Mom." I hiccupped the way I do when I cry too long.

"Cassie, what's wrong?"

"I want to go home, Mom. Please come take me home." I sniffled.

"Are you still not getting along with the girls in your cabin? I was hoping by now you'd have found a way to make friends."

Yeah, like that would ever happen.

"No, they still don't like me." I hiccupped again.

"Well, Cassie, you need to keep trying—"

"That's not it, Mom. It's...well...there's this boy." I walked around the corner of the building, pulling the cord after me, so the kids lined up to use the phone couldn't hear me.

"Oh, you're finally interested in boys—"

"No, Mom." I lowered my voice to a whisper. "This boy, Jason Bartlett, he keeps...bothering me."

"Bothering you? What do you mean?"

"Whenever I'm by myself, he shows up. He kisses me and touches me..." I let my voice trail off. I didn't know what else to say.

Mom coughed, then cleared her throat. "Cassie, sometimes young boys don't know the right way to tell a girl they like them. It's your job to make it clear that you're not that kind of girl. No touching allowed."

"It's not that easy, Mom. He's not a young boy. He's sixteen!"

Mom was quiet for so long I wondered if we'd gotten cut off. "What's this boy's name again?" she finally asked. I told her. "Okay," she said. "Don't worry. Daddy and I will take care of everything."

We said goodbye, and I nearly skipped back to the cabin. In just a few hours, I'd be home. Home. With my books and air conditioning and TV. School wouldn't start for two months. Two whole months without having to deal with any mean girls. Heaven.

A half-hour later, I sat on the basketball-court bleachers during the weekly sing-along. I'd picked a spot where I could see the one road that came into camp. I wanted to go pack the moment Mom and Dad arrived in our station wagon.

I was slapping a mosquito when I first heard the siren. It grew louder and louder. Then a police car roared in. Two officers got out and marched over to us. The singing trailed off, until all you could hear were the crickets and two little boys in the front who didn't notice they were the only ones still singing the "Oscar Mayer Wiener" song. A shush from their friends quickly shut them up, too.

Lenny and Fay, the head counselors, met the officers at the far edge of the chalkboard-green court. Moments later—while all the kids' mouths fell open—Lenny called Jason Bartlett over to speak with the police.

Oh, no. No no no. Mom hadn't called the police, had she? She was supposed to come take me home.

Fay stepped away from the officers and headed toward the bleachers. Toward me. "Cassie, can you come down here, please?"

Everyone gaped at me. My cheeks burned as I climbed down the bleachers. When I reached Fay, she put her arm around my shoulder and guided me away from the court. Jason, Lenny, and the police officers were headed to the camp office. Fay and I followed. It took two or three minutes. It felt like forever.

The sing-along started up again with the "Y.M.C.A." song as we entered the white cabin. It had air conditioning and padded window seats, and I wished I could be anywhere else. Fay guided me to one of the comfy spots. I flinched when Jason yelled "No way!" from behind a closed door.

Fay sat beside me, took my hand, and squeezed it. "Don't worry." She nodded at the door. "You're safe now. Why didn't you tell someone Jason was bothering you?"

I stared at my lap. What should I say? I never imagined Mom would call the police.

"I understand you told your mother that Jason has been touching you. Did he... He didn't...force you, did he?" Fay couldn't say the words, but I knew what she meant. Sort of.

My mouth felt desert dry. I scuffed my sneaker on the floor and mumbled that Jason and his friends had been making raids on our cabin late at night. At Fay's gasp, I looked up. Her tan had faded.

"Where has Gina been?"

My counselor. Right. I bowed my head again. "Um. She's a sound sleeper."

"And all the girls in your cabin are having this...problem?" Her voice sounded screechy. "Oh, my God." She gently placed her palm on my right cheek for a second before standing. "Stay right here, honey. You're safe here. I'm going to go get Gina and the rest of the girls."

"No!" I leapt up. "Please, I...I don't want them to know."

Fay turned and tilted her head. Some of her honey-blond hair escaped her ponytail. "What do you mean? How could they not know? You just said that the boys have been bothering them, too."

"Oh. That's right." My throat was parched, and I swallowed hard. "But the other girls...well, they might not remember."

Fay's eyes widened again as she put her hands on her hips. "Excuse me? I don't think I understand." But she did. I could see it in her eyes.

I sniffled as tears snaked down my cheeks and my chin trembled.

"Lenny," Fay called. "You should come out here."

"What's going on?" Lenny asked as he and the officers stepped into the room. They stopped short when they saw me crying.

"Cassie has something she wants to tell you." The chill in Fay's voice was worse than the camp lake early in the morning.

I crossed my arms across my chest. "I…I…" I stared at the floor. "I made it all up. I'm sorry. I didn't think my mom would tell anyone what I said. I just thought she'd come take me home. I want to go home."

When I looked up, I found Fay shaking her head and Lenny panting, his nostrils flaring like our neighbors' mean dog.

"You made it up?" Lenny said. "Do you have any idea what damage your accusation could have done?" He stormed toward me and pointed his finger in my face. "Your parents will be notified about all of this, and you are going to be punished for lying, young lady."

Jason barged into the room. "I told you I didn't do anything. Can I go now?" The cops shrugged and nodded. As Jason stomped out, the gray-haired officer checked his watch, then glared at me.

Maybe they would have sent me home if I hadn't already said how badly I wanted to leave. When my parents arrived minutes later—at first terrified and then furious—the grownups decided making me stay would be the best punishment. The story of what I'd done would spread like poison ivy. Facing Jason and everyone else each day would teach me not to tell tales anymore, my mom said. I think she might have been more understanding if I hadn't lied to her. That seemed to really piss her off.

My parents finally left, and I went back to my cabin and a whole new level of hell. My bunkmates had already heard what I'd accused Jason of by the time they returned from the sing-along. They talked about me as if I weren't there. The word *bitch* was used a lot.

I hoped things would soon return to normal, with the girls merely making fun of me. I'd find a way to put up with that for seven more weeks. But instead things got worse. During volleyball, everyone smacked the ball really hard at me. In the pool, girls kicked me as they swam by. And three mornings after I'd accused Jason, I woke up with wads of gum stuck in my hair. It took more than an hour to get it all out. A couple pieces, I had to cut out with Gina's scissors.

Gina punished Darla and her crew by taking away their afternoon snack, rainbow snow cones. But she didn't have much sympathy for me either. "You brought this on yourself," she'd said when she loaned me her scissors. "You're going to have to learn to deal with it." And the girls called *me* a bitch.

That night, our evening activity was again on the basketball court. Kids could get up and show off their talent. The girls from my cabin huddled near the bushes, practicing their cheers. Knowing I wasn't welcome, I took a seat on the end of a bleacher. An older girl sat next to me and elbowed me off the edge. I fell, scraping my knees. Gina sent me back to our cabin to clean up.

I walked gingerly under the pine trees. My right knee stung with each step, but I was happy to be alone for a while. Yet as I entered my empty cabin, I suddenly found myself fighting off tears. It was all too much. Why didn't anyone ever like me? I'd only had one good friend before, and she'd moved away two years ago. I slumped down on my springy bed, hugged my foam pillow to my chest, and squeezed my eyes shut.

Sometime later the cabin screen door screeched open. I wiped at my eyes. No way I'd let the girls see me cry. But they didn't come in. Jason Bartlett did. He pulled the wooden, inner door closed behind him, muffling the sound of a hooting owl.

"Hey. I saw you fall," he said. "How are you doing?"

"Okay." Why was he being nice to me?

He walked toward my bed. "I wanted to know, why'd you say that stuff about me?"

I bit my lip. My eyes started to tear again, and I dropped my chin on my chest. "I'm sorry. I shouldn't have said those things. I just wanted to go home. I never thought…"

My bedsprings creaked as he sat beside me, then lifted my chin with his thumb. "I guess you like me, huh?"

I started getting a funny feeling in my stomach. He was smiling at me in a way no one had ever smiled at me before.

Then his eyes turned mean. "And you think I like you back. What a loser." He leaned forward, licking his lips. "Let me show you what I like." He pushed down on top of me, tearing at my shorts. I tried to shove him away, but he was too strong.

A few minutes and several lifetimes later he got up. "That's what you get for accusing me, bitch. You better keep your mouth shut now." As he slammed the door behind him, I pulled up my shorts, then crawled under my gray blanket, shivering. I hurt in places I hadn't known could hurt.

When Gina and the girls finally came back, I crawled out of bed and tapped on Gina's arm. "I need to talk to you." I nodded my head toward the porch. She followed me outside.

I knew I should tell her what happened, but suddenly, I couldn't say anything.

Gina crossed her arms over her chest. "Well, what is it?"

"Umm." I took a deep breath and blinked away the tears welling up in my eyes. "While you were at the talent show, Jason Bartlett came here. He…he…"

A sigh escaped Gina's lips. "Bartlett, again? Really? What'd he do to you this time?"

I swallowed hard. "He forced me to...to, you know." I motioned toward my private area.

Her eyes widened. "You're telling me that Jason Bartlett came here and forced you to have sex with him?" I knew from the tone of her voice that she didn't believe me. "Okay. Tell me exactly what happened. Give me the details. If it's true, you'll be able to do that."

But I couldn't. I couldn't say those words. Relive it. I stared at the floor, silent.

"Just what I thought. I don't know why you're so hung up on Jason Bartlett, but you have got to stop making up lies about him. It's ridiculous."

Gina grabbed my elbow, pulled me to Fay's cabin, and told on me. Fay took away my snack-bar privileges for a week and marched me to Jason's cabin where she forced me to apologize.

Jason put on a good show, acting all mature and sympathetic for the little liar. But I saw the anger in his eyes.

A couple days later, while I was taking a shortcut through the woods, Jason jumped out from behind a tree. "You like to make trouble for me, don't you, loser? I'll show you trouble." I tried to run, but he was faster. If anyone noticed that my hair was full of pine needles and that the back of my shirt and shorts were smeared with dirt when I returned to the cabin, they didn't say anything.

I tried to stick around someone—anyone—after that, but the other kids were either mean to me or pretended I didn't exist, and Gina said she wouldn't be my babysitter. So sometimes I ended up alone. And every time that happened, Jason showed up.

By the time visiting day came at the end of July, my stomach was always in knots, and I jumped at the slightest sound. I couldn't stand it anymore. At least with the mean girls at home, I got a break after school every day. But here at camp, between the girls and Jason, the torture never ended. So as we sat on a scratchy wool blanket under the baking sun, I told Mom and Dad everything—well everything about the mean girls. I didn't dare tell them about Jason. No one ever believed me about him, and I didn't need to make things worse. I begged Mom and Dad to take me home. They looked at each other, communicating in that silent way of theirs, with head tilts and shakes, and said no. No. I must be exaggerating, Mom said. If I'd only try a little harder, I'd make friends. Besides, she wasn't raising a quitter. Then Dad told me to buck up, that this was the best time of my life. I started ripping up clumps of grass, fighting not to throw them.

"You look tired, Cassie," Mom said. "Go take a nap. I'm sure you'll feel better afterward. We'll see you in a few weeks."

In less than a minute, they packed up their cooler with the remains of our chicken-salad sandwiches, reminded me to write to my grandparents about the fun summer I was having, and left for the parking lot.

I stood there like road kill, watching them leave me without a backward glance. I'd told them I was miserable, and they didn't care. I began walking to my cabin, my fingernails slicing into my palms.

Why couldn't they ever stick up for me? Why did they always pretend things would be great if only I tried harder? Why didn't they ever get that my life wasn't the fairy tale they wanted it to be?

It took all my strength not to scream. Then I spotted Jason picnicking with his family. Smiling and laughing. I stared at him, my breaths coming in angry gasps, and something clicked inside my head. Suddenly I felt calmer. Everything seemed clearer. Kids were cruel. Grownups were useless. The only one I could count on was me, and I was done being everyone's punching bag.

I thought a moment, then headed for the woods.

That night after dinner, when all the happy families had left and my bunkmates played tetherball and did gymnastics, I went to the ceramics building. I had no real reason to go there—my bowl was still in the kiln. But I wanted to take the shortcut. And I wanted Jason to see me doing it.

I rushed through the woods, shaking. Except for that afternoon, when I knew Jason was busy with his parents, I hadn't been alone in the woods since that day he'd jumped me. I made it safely to the other side, then spent a few minutes in the ceramics building, taking deep breaths.

Soon I started back. Escaping the humid air, I hurried into the woods, where the trees' canopy kept the temperature cooler and the air drier. I started to tremble again as I stepped over fallen branches and reached the area where the ground was kind of level. Where Jason had surprised me before. My eyes darted left and right. The trees were so dense. Was he there?

A twig snapped, and I started as he sprung out from behind a huge oak. His eyes gleamed while a horrifying smirk creased his face.

My whole body shook as he came at me, leaves and pine needles crunching under foot. I started to run, but after just a few steps, he tackled me.

"Aw, why are you making things hard on yourself?"

I tried to crawl away. I got maybe a yard before he grabbed me again and flipped me over. While he unzipped his jean shorts, I squirmed backward. I'd only moved a few inches before he yanked down my shorts, pressed on me, and the pain began again.

I flailed my hands around while he grunted. Oh, God. Where were the rocks? The rocks I'd scattered around, because I'd figured Jason would choose this spot again. I stretched until I thought I'd dislocate my shoulder. Finally my hand brushed one. I twisted and slipped my fingers around it.

The rock was rough and sharp. Heavy. Eyes closed, I took a deep breath and slammed it against the back of Jason's head. He shuddered, and I hit him again and again and again. He dropped down on me. The whole world seemed to stop.

Was he breathing? I listened closely. No. I couldn't hear him anymore. All I could hear were the birds singing in the twilight and my own heart beating ferociously.

I shoved Jason off, nearly vomited, then pulled my shorts up. I couldn't take my eyes off him. He was dead. Had to be. Arms shaky, I leaned over and pushed his thing back in his jeans and zipped them up. I grabbed the rock. It had blood and some of Jason's hair on it. I threw it as far as I could into the woods. Then I took some deep breaths, shook the twigs and leaves from my hair, and brushed myself off before starting back.

I'd done it. I was free.

I felt stunned with those first few steps, surprised I'd pulled it off. Then happiness surged through me. I began laughing as I shoved away a low-lying branch, ripping its leaves off and throwing them in the air. Free! Score one for the little liar. No one was ever going to fuck with me again and get away with it.

I composed myself before I left the woods and went back to my cabin to read. Not that I could concentrate. I kept waiting for all hell to break loose. It started slowly. After Jason missed the evening activity, some counselors began searching for him. Then more did. And more. But they didn't find him until the next day. Not until some animals and a lot of insects had feasted on him. Word quickly spread about the state of Jason's body. Some girls cried.

Not me.

The police arrived soon after. A lot of them. All the kids stayed on their cabin porches, peeking at the woods as best they could. The cops were in there a long time. Finally, some of them came out and headed to the camp office. They must have asked if anyone had a grudge against Jason because within minutes Lenny came and got me, his nostrils flaring again.

"You're an evil little girl, aren't you," he said as he marched me to the camp office.

I'm what you all made me, asshole.

I shoved my hands in my pockets to hide the scratches from the twigs and pine needles and kept talking to myself.

You can do this. Stay strong. Don't let them get to you.

My heart thudded so loudly as we neared the office, I was sure the whole camp could hear. But as I stumbled across the threshold—thanks to a little push from Lenny—a cop with a red mustache shook his head.

"This is the girl you told us about?" he asked Lenny, rolling his eyes.

Lenny nodded.

"Nah. No way she could've done it. She's way too small. The boy was hit from behind near the top of his head. Whoever did it must have been much taller. Go round up the older kids and the counselors. They're the ones we want to talk to."

I fought not to smirk. Being short had finally paid off.

I practically floated back to my cabin, feeling stronger than I ever had before. Invincible. Then I saw Darla standing on the porch, giving me the evil eye. I gave it right back to her.

One down. One to go. And then I'd take care of the head bitch back home.

I laughed out loud. Dad was right. This was going to be the time of my life.

※

I once heard an editor say that she loved stories with interesting, unusual settings. I live in the suburbs. Haven't traveled much. I wondered if I could I create a setting that isn't the same-old same-old? And then I thought of sleep-away camp. I went to a wonderful sleep-away camp in Connecticut as a kid. I remember the smell of the grass, the songs, the sports, the friendships, and the girl you couldn't stand (until she came back the next summer and became your best friend—had I changed or had she?). That was the world I wanted to re-create in "Evil Little Girl." Where the plot came from, I'm not quite sure. It's certainly not autobiographical, except for the title. In the third grade, I got into an argument with my best friend. I then tattled on her to our school librarian. I'll never forget how the librarian looked at me and said, "You're an evil little girl, aren't you?" I can't remember the librarian's name, but her words have stuck with me. I'm glad I'm finally able to put them to good use. And Mrs. X, wherever you are, don't worry. I've turned out just fine. Okay, I kill people for a living, but it's fictional, so I hope we're all good.

MURDER AT SLEUTHFEST

Mother was always vigilant about hygiene. Someone sneezes near you, wash your hands. Leave the house and touch anything, wash your hands. And don't just wash them, scrub them. When I got older and started wearing rings, Mother trained me to remove them when I washed. Mustn't let germs hide beneath the band.

Even now, with the advent of Purell and Mother dead a good twenty-five years, I'd wash my hands thirty times a day if I could. I might not have noticed the effects of the disease so early if I weren't meticulous. The slight tremor in my fingers might have escaped me five years ago if I hadn't paid so much attention when I scrubbed.

I'd never have known back then that the disease that killed Mother had come for me, too.

Three kids in my family, but I'm the one who watched her die. My brother, Dave, is a Manhattan shrink. When we realized Mother was becoming helpless, he had a kid and an extravagant wife to support. No way he could afford a sabbatical from work. Marion, my little sis, was in law school. We told her not to take time away from school. She happily obliged. Mother had imposed a fear of germs on Marion, too. So much so that when Mother got the disease, Marion shied away, even though it's not catching.

That left me. The unmarried mystery writer. I could practice my craft from anywhere, and I had nobody to leave behind. So I packed up and moved back home to Philly. To Mother's sterile house. And I watched the disease attack her muscles, destroying her mobility and, in turn, her dignity. Until the day she couldn't swallow anymore. She refused a feeding tube. We buried her two weeks later.

The doctors told us the disease wasn't hereditary. They didn't know the cause, but they knew that.

I didn't believe them.

After noticing my first symptom, I felt vindicated, in a sick sort of way. The doctors treated me like a hypochondriac when I showed up and claimed the rare disease as my own. Now that I can't type my stories anymore, that I can't wash anymore, that I can hardly move and have to recite this in my wobbly voice, now they believe me.

But I knew from that first tremor. And I knew I didn't want to die like Mother did.

So I hatched a plan and in March headed off to the annual Sleuthfest mystery conference in Fort Lauderdale. I met up with old pals, and over a round of margaritas, I pitched my next book. It'd involve a murder for hire. I wanted to make it authentic. Who could I speak with for details? They shared names of cops. But I wanted someone on the inside, I said. My friend Gabby came through. Her town had a big case like that a few years back. She recalled the killer's name and where he sat on death row.

I sent a letter of introduction the next morning. It didn't take long for the guy to agree to see me. Guess he wanted company. Securing official permission to visit him took longer. Finally I got it. By my third visit we were old chums. That's when I revealed my plan. I needed someone in his line of work. Could he help me?

I know I would've saved a lot of time and trouble if I'd just killed myself, but Mother had raised me to be squeamish. I simply couldn't.

It was the next February when I finally struck the deal with Rex. I never knew his real name. We made all our contact using pay phones. I felt devious, like a character in my books. That made me feel better.

Rex didn't want me to see his face, and I agreed. I feared I wouldn't be able to go through with it if I spotted him, knowing what was coming. I sent him payment in cash to a post office box. We resolved it should happen not in my town or his. And then I thought of Sleuthfest. I hadn't planned to go that year. The disease had progressed steadily, and I couldn't climb stairs anymore, had trouble opening doors. Moving hurt. But it seemed the perfect place. With all those people milling about the hotel, Rex could come and go without being noticed. It'd be easy. And it had style. Murder at a mystery conference.

Rex didn't know exactly what I looked like. The photo on my books had been taken ten years and twenty pounds ago. I offered to send a current picture, but he said no. He didn't want to risk anyone he knew seeing it. Might connect him with me. The old photo on the library book would be good enough. So I told him my brown hair now had streaks of gray. I said I'd wear the gaudiest ring I owned. A big fake diamond surrounded by large imitation sapphires and rubies. It'd be on my left ring finger. He couldn't miss it.

After the first session of the conference, I headed to the ladies room. Had to wash my hands. I removed the ring while I scrubbed and forgot to put it back on. Left it sitting next to the sink.

I realized my blunder fifteen minutes later. By the time I made it back to the restroom, the ring was gone. I hoped a kind soul had found it and turned it in at the hotel's front desk. Nope. I had announcements made in each session for the rest of the day. A ring with a large diamond surrounded by sapphires and rubies was left in the women's restroom. Great sentimental value. Please return it if you found it. I even offered a $100 reward.

I prayed the thief would be smart enough not to slip it on during the conference.

No such luck.

A scream interrupted the last session that day. A woman had been found dead in the silent auction room at the end of the hall. She'd been shot at close range, her blood soiling the beige carpeting onto which she'd crumpled. She was an unpublished author, I learned. Searching for an agent. Her hair was brown and graying like mine. And there, on her left ring finger, sat my ring.

The police questioned me, being the owner of the stolen ring, but my alibi was solid. I eventually got the ring back. I don't wear it.

I never spoke with Rex again. As far as I know, the Fort Lauderdale police never solved the murder of the woman who stole my ring.

And I sit here in my wheelchair, straining to breathe, unable to move, waiting to die. After the conference, I decided this should be my punishment. My punishment for being so scared of the disease. So scared my plan might be discovered that I let a thief be murdered.

I just wish I could wash my hands one more time.

☙

"Murder at Sleuthfest" first appeared in Chesapeake Crimes II, *originally published by Quiet Storm Press in 2005. This story was nominated for the 2005 Agatha Award.*

When I wrote "Murder at Sleuthfest," I'd been working on a mystery novel for a while, but I hadn't written any short stories since high school. (Let's not talk about those beauties.) In fact, I'd never published any crime fiction. But I was inspired: I had attended the Sleuthfest mystery conference earlier that year, where my lovely diamond-and-sapphire ring was stolen. (I bear no ill will against the conference organizers; I'm the dope who took off my ring and left it on a bathroom sink in the hotel, from where someone pocketed it.) If I was going to lose that ring, I was going to ensure something good came out of it. So I devised this story, setting it at Sleuthfest, where someone steals a ring and gets her just dessert. The result was my first published story, and it was nominated for an Agatha Award, too, which was amazing icing on the cake. While I wish I had gotten the ring back, the theft is what ultimately inspired me to begin writing short stories, and for that, I'm actually, somewhat, grateful.

TRUTH AND CONSEQUENCES

"We discussed prostitution, adultery, and drug use in school today," I announced at dinner. "Did you know they're victimless crimes?"

My mother nearly choked on her green beans. "You what?"

"It was all Andy Telwacht's fault. He and Robbie Winters did their oral debate in Social Studies on marijuana. Robbie called it a gateway drug and said people should go to jail for a long time for using it. Then Andy said that smoking pot didn't hurt anyone, and it should be legal here in Illinois just like it is in Europe!"

Dad's eyes bugged out while Mom's face turned a deep red. Boy, I loved to get them going.

"You know how Mr. Carracio always tells us to 'think for ourselves,'" I went on. "So we got into this big debate about whether marijuana is dangerous. Bonnie Kingman said it's not, that it's just like prostitution and adultery. If everyone's a consenting adult, what's the problem? I kind of think she's right."

Mom slapped the table top so hard, my plate of chicken bounced. "This is what we get for spending our hard-earned money on that fancy private school."

She scowled and wagged her finger at me. "You listen to me, Cara. Drug use, prostitution, and adultery are not victimless crimes. People get hurt in ways you can't even begin to fathom when you're fourteen years old. If you even think about doing drugs and I find out about it—and believe me, I will—you will rue the day."

I rolled my eyes. Rue the day. Mom was so melodramatic.

* * * *

An hour later, Dad poked his head in my room. His curly brown hair fell across his forehead, covering his eyebrows. He looked so dorky. I tugged off my iPod earbuds.

"Mom and I are going to the supermarket," he said. "She wants ice cream. I'll turn on the alarm on the way out."

"Okay," I said. "See you later."

I tried to play it cool, but I was psyched. Now I could ditch my algebra homework for something far more important: searching for my Christmas presents. Ten days till Christmas. No way I could wait that long to see what this year's haul would be. Over the last week, I'd hunted around the house for my gifts. I'd only found one: a black and gray Dooney & Bourke wristlet buried in a Tupperware container. Mom's been real sneaky about hiding my presents since fifth grade, when she caught me searching for them. Boy, had she yelled that day.

"Cara Beth Holloway, what do you think you're doing?"

I was elbow-deep in her underwear drawer. What did she think I was doing?

"You get out of this room right now, young lady. Snooping can be dangerous business."

Yeah, right. I couldn't imagine what I might possibly discover that would be dangerous. My parents simply weren't that interesting.

Now, with them out for probably an hour, I concentrated my search on their bedroom. Every nook and cranny had to be systematically examined. Mom's stealth knew no bounds.

Unfortunately, after a half hour, I still hadn't found anything meant for me. Dad had apparently bought cruise tickets for him and Mom (which meant—please no—that my grandparents would come to watch me while they were gone). Where was my stuff? I really wanted that new phone Kim got for her birthday. It's tiny. It could be hidden anywhere.

I decided to hit the closet by the front door. I hadn't checked there yet. I rifled through every pocket of every coat. Nothing.

Then I reached down to the snow shoes we kept in the back of the closet. Maybe Mom had slipped something inside one of them.

I was on my knees when I heard keys in the front door. Oh, no! I quickly snuggled back behind the coats and had almost pulled the closet door shut when Mom and Dad came in. I crooked my head sideways, peering through the crack.

"You really think she'll like them?" Mom whispered, holding a bag from Jake, one of the hottest stores here in Winnetka.

I nearly hyperventilated. My boots! They had to be the black suede boots I wanted!

"Of course she'll like them," Dad said. "She has the same expensive tastes you do, and these boots cost a fortune."

He pulled the closet door open, and I nearly hyperventilated again. How would I explain hiding in the closet? If they caught me, Mom might just return the boots to teach me a lesson. She loved doing things like that. I held my breath and tried not to move as Dad reached in and grabbed a hanger.

"Oh, before I forget," Mom said.

Dad looked over his shoulder.

"The coat I ordered for Cara has come in," Mom said. "I need you to pick it up tomorrow."

Coat? What coat?

Dad shoved his jacket in the closet and turned, shaking his head back and forth like he always does when he starts getting aggravated. "Why can't you do it?"

I took a breath as quietly as possible as Dad snatched another hanger and shoved Mom's fur-trimmed coat on the rack. It pushed up against my nose, which began tickling.

"Why can't *I* do it?" Mom said. "Because I have a hair appointment, Christmas is right around the corner, and the store's at Northbrook Court. You'll be heading that way anyway. Won't you?" Mom's tone made clear she knew the answer was yes.

I swallowed several times, trying to smother the sneeze that now desperately wanted out.

"You know how limited my time is on Saturdays," Dad said. "And I won't be able to go at all next weekend, what with the relatives coming to visit."

"I don't want to hear it, Bill. Cara never gets any of your time on Saturday afternoons. This is the least you can do for her."

If I didn't know better, I'd think they were drawing out this conversation to make me suffer. Heck, maybe they were.

"Fine," Dad said, shutting the closet door. "I've got to get this ice cream into the freezer before it melts."

I waited a few seconds, wrinkling and rubbing my nose, then let out a huge breath. That was close. I waited another thirty seconds before inching the door open. The coast was clear.

As I snuck back to my room, I wondered yet again what kept Dad busy each Saturday. He always left around lunchtime to "run errands" and came home hours later with a bag of bagels and the *Chicago Tribune*. I asked to go along once when I was little, but he said no, that he had important, secret work to do. I'd decided then that he was a spy. But of course that couldn't be true. No way Dad could fix people's teeth during the week and be a spy on the weekends. And I knew he really was a dentist. I'd suffered in his chair more than once.

So what was this important, secret work? And why would it piss off Mom? My snooping gene in overdrive, I decided I finally had to find out. Besides, it might give me the chance to check out my new coat at the same time. Maybe it was suede, too, and matched my boots!

A knock on my bedroom door interrupted my coat fantasy. "Come in."

"Just wanted to let you know that we're home, honey," Mom said, leaning against the door frame. "We bought some of your favorite strawberry ice cream, in case you want any."

"Yum! Thanks. Hey, I made plans to go over to Kim's tomorrow. FYI."

"Okay. Do you want a ride?"

"No. It's just a few blocks. The exercise will be good for me. I can work off the ice cream I'm going to eat."

Mom smiled. "Sweet dreams, then. I'm getting in bed with my ice cream and my *People* magazine."

Once I heard her bedroom door close, I called my best friend, Kim. She agreed to be my cover for the next day, after making me promise to give her all the details of my spy mission.

With a plan in place, I sat at the kitchen table with a small dish of ice cream and my algebra homework. Dad always pushed me to get my assignments done Friday night, so I wouldn't have to worry about them all weekend long. I tried to finish the math, but I honestly couldn't care less about figuring out what X stood for. I had a bigger puzzle on my mind.

* * * *

My alarm woke me at 11 o'clock the next morning. Most weekend days, I sleep till noon. While I hated giving up my catch-up sleep—on school days I have to get up at the obscene hour of six—satisfying my curiosity would be worth it. I took a quick, twenty-minute shower, dressed, blew my hair dry, grabbed some PowerBars, and headed out.

But instead of walking over to Kim's, I got in the back of Dad's blue Lexus and burrowed under the old blanket on the backseat. Mom was going through "the change," and some-times she'd get really hot and switch on the car air conditioner, even if it was twenty degrees outside! So Dad left a blanket on the back seat for me to use during family car rides.

I texted with Kim for a few minutes. When I heard Dad's keys jingling, I jammed the phone's off button, plunged onto the floor behind Dad's seat, and focused on staying still and breathing lightly. I prayed the crumpled blanket didn't attract Dad's attention.

Moments later Dad climbed behind the wheel, turned on the radio, and off we went. He hadn't noticed me. Score!

We drove for about fifteen minutes, accompanied by a Beatles marathon. (Could my dad be more lame?) I could tell when we reached the mall because Dad started muttering about the traffic and all the holiday shoppers. It sounded like he circled a bit before he finally found a spot and headed in. I waited a few seconds after he left the car to throw off the blanket and peek out the window. He'd parked by the movie theater. That would mean my coat might come from Abercrombie & Fitch. Or Ann Taylor. Did they sell coats? Or…please, please, please…maybe Mom bought me a coat from CUSP. It's the coolest store ever.

I nibbled on a PowerBar while I kept my eyes peeled on the mall entrance. Finally, about ten minutes later, Dad came out with a bag from…oh, my God! CUSP! My life couldn't get any better. Any coat from CUSP would be totally fab. My friends would be so jealous!

I curled up under the blanket again just before Dad got in the car and tossed the CUSP bag on the front passenger seat. Soon we were off again. I meant to pay attention to where we were going, but I kept thinking about ways I could peek at my coat. I couldn't stand waiting nine more days.

Maybe twenty minutes later, the car stopped again. Dad got out, and it sounded like he lifted the trunk lid, then slammed it shut. When he didn't get back in the car, I slipped the blanket off my head, brushing my hair from my face. Jeez, it had gotten hot under there. I glanced out the window. We were in a townhouse complex with bare trees surrounding the parking lot. Dad was heading for an end unit, carrying some wrapped gifts.

What kind of errand was this?

I noticed the CUSP bag still on the front passenger seat and shifted toward it while I kept my eyes on Dad. He reached the door, pulled out a key, and let himself in.

What the...

The coat could wait. I shot out of the car, dashed to the house's front window, and on tippy toes peered inside. A woman with long blond hair was putting most of Dad's gifts under a stubby Christmas tree with white lights. And there was Dad, hugging some kid with curly brown hair.

The kid seemed a few years younger than me and kind of looked familiar. Dad handed him one of the gifts, he tore it open, and smiled. I sucked in my breath when he did, because I knew that smile. Dad's smile. The kid hugged him again, and even though I couldn't read lips very well, the kid's next words clearly were, "Thanks, Daddy."

A brother?

I had a brother?

I spun away from the window and rubbed my hand over my face. Dad wasn't a spy. He was a bigamist. Or an adulterer. Or something else awful. I'd always wanted a brother or sister but not like this. I'd have to tell Mom. I sagged against the building. Wait. Mom must already know. She knows how Dad leaves every Saturday. That's what they argued about last night.

I slid down against the side of the house. The aluminum siding's coldness seeped straight through my jacket, into my bones. This couldn't be happening. I live in Winnetka. In a nice house. With my parents. Both of them. We're a normal family. No problems. And Christmas is coming. I'm going to get great gifts. Like every year. No way Dad is leading a double life. No way he has another kid. I'm his kid. His only kid. I must have made a mistake.

I scrambled up, went to the door, and knocked before I lost my nerve. The blond woman opened the door a moment later and gasped. Then Dad gasped, too.

"Who's that girl, Daddy?" the kid asked.

Wow. I wasn't the only one who'd been lied to.

"Cara!" Dad rushed to the door. "What are you doing here?"

I was breathing heavily. "I wanted to see my coat and find out where you went all the time, so I hid in the back seat. I wanted to be in on the big secret. Please tell me this is all a joke, Dad. Right? You're his Big Brother or something like that? Right? We learned about that in school. That's a really nice thing to do. Or you're here doing community service. Dental house calls? Is that it? There's got to be an explanation."

I was talking too fast. Maybe if I kept talking, I'd come up with a good reason why this was happening.

Dad grabbed my arms. "Cara, calm down." He shook me a little until I focused on him. "You weren't supposed to find out this way. Your mother and I decided to wait until you were older. Until you could handle it."

"Handle what?" It took all my strength not to cry. "What's going on?"

Eyes darting between me and the kid, Dad appeared on the verge of tears, too. He pulled me toward the couch set against the wall, then waved the kid over to us. His hair was the same shade of brown as Dad's. And mine.

Chin quivering, Dad focused on me. "Cara, this is your brother, Michael." He turned to the kid. "Michael…you have a big sister. Her name is Cara."

The kid looked as freaked out as I felt.

"What?" The kid whipped his head back and forth between Dad and the blond lady. "Mommy, what's Daddy mean? A sister? I don't get it."

Snooping can be dangerous business. Mom's voice echoed in my head.

The blond woman came over and held out her hand. "Michael, let's go to your room so I can explain some things." Her voice shook a little.

The kid turned and stared at me for a minute, then took her hand. As they headed down a hallway, I noticed a bunch of pictures on the wall, including one of Dad and the kid. Swallowing hard, I turned my attention to the faded blue and yellow flower print on the couch until Dad lifted my chin with his finger.

"Your mom and I had some problems when you were little. And I made some mistakes. Jocelyn," he nodded toward the bedroom, "used to be my dental hygienist." Dad sighed. "I guess you're old enough to hear this now....Well, we had an affair." He scrunched his eyes closed for a second and shook his head. "It didn't last very long. I realized how much I love your mom and broke it off, but by then Michael was on the way."

I didn't want to know about this. I kept thinking about my new coat and boots. If I kept thinking about them, surely this would all go away.

"It took a long time for your mom to forgive me," Dad continued. "And she's been very supportive all these years, letting me come here every Saturday to spend time with your brother. He's a great kid. You're going to love him."

Love him? I didn't even know him.

Lots of my friends' parents were divorced, but I'd never worried about that. I thought Mom and Dad were happy. But how happy could they be with this big secret in their lives? It must be so hard on Mom knowing Dad spends every Saturday with this other family. With this woman that he... I shook my head. I couldn't go there. How could Dad have this other life all these years and I never knew? How could he have done this to Mom? To us?

And Mom. My God. How could she have accepted this? How could she have forgiven him?

How could I?

"You're growing up, Cara," Dad said. "You're fourteen now. It's time you learned life isn't always nice and tidy. But we can make this work." He paused. "How I'm going to explain this to your mother is another story."

I stared at him, my eyes watering. What would I tell Kim? I'd have to make something up. She couldn't know. No one could know. It's one thing for parents to divorce, marry other people, and then have more kids. But to have an affair and a child like this. And to hide it for years. Everyone would talk about me if they knew. All the kids would laugh or point or whisper.

"Please, honey. It's nearly Christmas. If you could try to accept your brother, it would be the best present in the world to me."

My heart said no, but I felt my head nodding yes. Dad hugged me.

"Thank you, Cara. This is going to work out. You'll see. No more secrets. Finally, I'll be able to spend time with you and Michael together as a family."

Great, family togetherness with a stranger.

I laid my head on Dad's shoulder and felt the first tears slide from my eyes as I tried to make sense of it all. Unbelievable that just a half hour before, a new suede coat and boots had me on top of the world.

Bonnie Kingman didn't know what she was talking about. Mom was right, there's no such thing as a victimless crime.

What a crock.

※

"Truth and Consequences" first appeared in Mystery Times Ten, *published by Buddhapuss Ink in 2011. This story was nominated for the 2011 Agatha Award and the 2012 Anthony and Macavity awards.*

As a child, I loved sneaking around my house, pretending to be a spy, taking photos, and trying to overhear dastardly plots (or at least scare my mother). There never were any plots, but I did make Mom jump quite a few times. It was that fun experience (yes, I have a sadistic side) that inspired this story. I'd like to give thanks to my niece Kelsey Goffman, who helped me with the suburban Chicago shopping details.

VOLUNTEER OF THE YEAR

"Ladies and gentlemen, the Buckaroo Ball is pleased to honor this year's volunteer of the year, Gaylene Banks."

As the applause began, I took a deep breath and made my way to the microphone. The hot stage lights burned so brightly I couldn't see anyone in the audience. But I knew my husband, Gavin, sat at the honorees' table front and center, likely nursing his second gin and tonic. Heck, maybe his third.

My heart began beating erratically as I started to speak. I didn't know if it was anxiety or my cardiac arrhythmia acting up.

Calm down, Gaylene. It's only nerves. Everything's going to work out just fine.

I inhaled deeply once again, soon got into a rhythm, and the speech flew by. Mother would have been proud if she'd lived to see this day. I was poised and elegant. Not a hair on my silver head slipped from its place. My white pearl necklace and button earrings added the perfect touch to my stylish black dress. Granted I'd dressed up more than nearly all the other women, who favored casual, southwestern attire. But all eyes were on me, not them.

Like a good Buckaroo, I hit all the right notes in my speech. The importance of working in the community. Of protecting children. Of giving back. I touted the Buckaroo Ball. How it's the biggest annual charity event in New Mexico. I thanked everyone in the audience who had given their time and money to help the Buckaroo Ball Committee aid the at-risk children of Santa Fe County. And I gave a nod to my husband, who had supported me all these years, enabling me to volunteer full time—and then some—to help abused children, long before the Buckaroo Ball Committee came into existence.

I'd debated whether to mention Gavin in my speech. I'd worked so hard to keep him apart from my volunteer life. But in the end I realized I couldn't avoid it, not without raising eyebrows. And that just wouldn't do.

An hour later, Gavin twirled me around the dance floor. He was larger than life, his black Stetson casting a shadow over his twinkling blue eyes. He smelled a bit like his favorite horse, as usual, no matter how much he showered.

"Congratulations, Gaylene," Bitsy Allen called as she two-stepped nearby. "They couldn't have picked a better person to honor. And it's wonderful to finally meet your husband. He's a doll."

"Why thank you, pretty lady." Gavin tipped his hat. "Perhaps later this evening, you'd give me the honor of a dance."

"You got it, sugar," Bitsy said.

Yes, everybody always loved Gavin. He knew how to turn on the charm.

It was Gavin who spurred me to get involved in children's causes forty-five years ago. At the time, we'd been married just a couple years. I'd come home a day early from visiting Mother and Daddy in Dallas. Gavin surely was surprised to see me. He hustled little Tommy Greenley out of our den, pretending everything was normal, calling after Tommy to keep working on his batting swing. Tommy looked scared. Wouldn't meet my eyes. Gavin had been coaching Tommy's Little League team, but that wasn't baseball going on in the den.

I left Gavin that night, but I couldn't make it stick. In the 1960s, you didn't talk about things like that. And you didn't leave your husband. So I moved back home a few days later, after Gavin promised to quit coaching. To quit having anything to do with kids. To focus all his time on the ranch. I moved into the spare bedroom, began volunteering with children's causes to make myself feel better, and settled into a quiet, celibate existence.

That was probably my mistake, I realize now. Gavin needed some release. And I'd denied him.

"Gaylene, honey, where's your mind?" Gavin drew me closer than I ever let him in private. "You haven't heard a word I said."

I smiled up at him, shrugged my shoulders. He'd been my dream come true when we met in 1961. I was an eighteen-year-old freshman at Southern Methodist University, ready for my happily ever after. A husband, a home, a family. Gavin was in his senior year. A football star. We had a six-month, whirlwind courtship before we wed. I dropped out of school, we moved to a house outside Santa Fe, and Gavin began working on his family's cattle ranch.

Mother flew out a few times the first year of our marriage, helping me make our house a home while Gavin worked long hours. We even decorated a nursery that looked out on a large pasture dotted with cottonwood trees. But it sat empty.

Thank God.

The song finally ended. I made my way to an empty table while Gavin headed to the bar.

"There she is, our volunteer of the year," Freddy Crawford said as he and his wife joined me. "I don't think I've ever seen a prettier gal, except for my Miranda here, of course." He pecked his wife on the cheek as she sat down.

She laughed and patted my hand. "Honey, it's good to see your husband supporting you at one of these functions. He's missed so many over the years, we were beginning to wonder if he was a spy or something, leading a secret life somewhere else."

"A secret life?" I laughed back.

Miranda leaned forward, her jasmine perfume tickling my nose. "You know, it wasn't till he started volunteering at the YMCA some months back that I knew Gavin shared any of your interests in children's causes. He's been such a help with the afternoon tutoring and the sports programs."

I forced myself to smile. It was Miranda who'd first mentioned Gavin's volunteering to me a few weeks ago during one of our charity luncheons. Then Deborah Paterson piped in that the Boy Scouts were grateful for all of Gavin's support, too—time and money.

How I hadn't known about his renewed extra-curricular activities, I don't know. Maybe I hadn't wanted to know. In the beginning, Gavin seemed to live up to his promise, burying himself in helping run his daddy's ranch. After a while, I'd busied myself so much with my charities that I'd stopped paying attention to what Gavin was doing.

But after listening to Miranda and Deborah, I couldn't stay blind anymore.

I spotted Gavin heading our way and jumped up. "Time to cha-cha. Gavin is just a dancing fool." I hurried over and drew him out on the floor.

"Since when do you like to dance so much?" he asked about ten minutes later, stepping in time with me to a Texas waltz.

"Since you're here in public with me, making a good appearance."

When the song ended, Gavin wanted to take another breather, but I pressed for one more dance. The band had started a real fast one. Gavin might have been in his late sixties and a bit pudgy, but he still could tear up the floor. So much so that we attracted a small audience, which spurred Gavin to keep going for three more numbers.

By the time we took a break, he was sweating something fierce. "Gavin, honey, you don't look so good. You go sit down. I'll get you some water."

"Scotch," he said as he fanned his face with his hat.

I sidled up to the empty end of the bar, set my purse on the counter, and ordered Gavin's drink. The music caught my attention, and I turned around, taking in the room. Everyone looked so wonderful. Bitsy spotted me and waved. Lord, was she fixing to come over here?

"Here you go, ma'am." The bartender set down Gavin's scotch.

"Can I also get a Long Island iced tea, please?"

While the bartender went off to make the seven-liquor drink, I put my cell phone to my ear, pretending I was on a call. I didn't want anyone, especially Bitsy, to bother me. She's nice, but boy, could she talk.

I waited a few seconds and glanced over my shoulder. Good. No Bitsy. Never one to have idle hands, I began fiddling in my purse. When my drink finally arrived, I snapped my purse shut, switched off the phone, and headed back to our table, still swirling Gavin's scotch.

"Here you go. One scotch." I beamed at him while he gulped it down. "Whoa, that's kind of fast, honey. You want another?"

"You're being awful nice to me tonight, Gaylene."

"It's my night. I want everything to go just right."

I got him another scotch, which he downed, too. A few minutes later, Gavin leaned over. "I think I'm gonna be sick."

I sprang up. "Well don't do it here in the middle of the room."

I yanked him to his feet and walked him to the men's room, his breathing shallow. He headed in, and I entered the ladies' room. Calm, as if nothing unusual was going on.

"Congratulations again, Gaylene." Bitsy sat next to me at the vanity while I touched up my face. "That sure is a pretty color lipstick. And I loved your speech tonight. I'm always in awe of you and everything you do for children. There doesn't seem to be any task you're not willing to take on."

I smiled. "Thank you, Bitsy. You're so very sweet."

A commotion nearly overwhelmed me when I left the ladies' room.

"Gaylene! There you are!" Freddy Crawford grabbed my arms. "We've called the paramedics. Gavin passed out in the bathroom."

"Oh, my Lord." Forsaking my sense of propriety, I barged into the men's room. Tyler Harrison was giving Gavin CPR. How lucky that a doctor was in the restroom when Gavin collapsed.

"Tyler, what's going on?" I knelt next to Gavin, who now smelled more like vomit than horse. "Will he be all right? What happened?"

Tyler kept pushing on Gavin's chest, his face grim. "How much did he have to drink tonight?"

"Um, I'm not sure. Two or three gin and tonics at the beginning of the night. Then at some point he switched to scotch. Might have had a couple bourbons, too."

"He always drink that much?"

"Yes. But he's never had any trouble before."

"Any history of heart problems?"

"No. You think it's his heart?" I pressed my hand to my own, feeling it beat rapidly in my chest. "Oh, no! His daddy died of a heart attack."

I slumped back against the wall while Freddy hurried the rest of the men out of the room. Then he sat down beside me and took my hand.

Tyler put his ear to Gavin's lips, his fingers to Gavin's neck. Shook his head. When he resumed chest compressions a moment later, Tyler looked defeated. Gavin was pale. I didn't sense any life left in him.

Tears filled my eyes while Freddy patted my hand. "He's gonna be all right. You'll see." The bathroom door banged open as the paramedics sped in, followed by some firefighters and a police officer. I swallowed hard. The room suddenly felt very crowded.

"You've got an overweight man, late sixties to early seventies, apparent heart attack," Tyler said while they took over Gavin's care. "I've done CPR for the last five minutes or so."

"He's sixty-nine," I said, my voice squeaking.

"He collapsed here," Tyler went on. "Vomited first. Looks like he drank too much tonight and overdid it on the dance floor."

"No pulse," the red-haired paramedic said. A fireman hooked Gavin up to a heart monitor, while the redhead took over the CPR. The other paramedic interrupted a few times to shock Gavin. Then someone shoved a tube attached to a ventilation bag down Gavin's throat. Someone else started an IV. I tried to back away.

"We've got to hurry," the redhead said as he and his partner loaded Gavin on a stretcher.

I struggled to my feet to follow the paramedics as they rushed out of the restroom with Gavin, but I staggered. Freddy, bless him, steadied me.

"You okay?" he asked.

I exhaled a deep breath. "Yes. I think so."

"You're gonna have to run to go with the ambulance, Gaylene," Freddy said. "Miranda and I can take you to the hospital. Why don't you let us do that?"

I nodded. "Thank you, Freddy. A ride would be good." My breath became a bit ragged as I fought off tears. "I'd just like a minute to myself first."

"Of course. Tyler and I'll wait outside."

Freddy and Tyler left the restroom, leaving me all alone. I headed to one of the stalls. Thankfully it was clean. I'd always heard horror stories about men's rooms.

I reached into my purse and pulled out the baggie I had packed that afternoon. Just a trace of my crushed heart pills remained inside. I tossed the baggie into the toilet and flushed twice, making sure the evidence floated away.

My tears started flowing then. Tears of relief. And sadness. I wiped my cheek with the back of my hand.

Yes, it was my special night. And Bitsy was right. I'd do anything to keep children safe.

Anything.

※

"Volunteer of the Year" first appeared in Chesapeake Crimes: They Had It Comin', *published by Wildside Press in 2010. This story was nominated for the 2010 Agatha Award.*

I once read a short story where a crime was committed right before the reader's eyes, but it was disguised so well by the author, I didn't realize the crime had happened until the end of the story. I was intrigued by that twist and wanted to see if I could do it myself. That was the premise behind "Volunteer of the Year." Many thanks to New Mexico-based author Christine Barber, who helped me get the details about the paramedics correct. Any mistakes, of course, are my own.

THE CONTEST

John swiped my suntan lotion off my desk as he strode toward the newsroom door.

"I'm off to do a Suzy Q special, interviewing some of those college girls working the boardwalk concession stands," he called over his shoulder, an annoying grin creasing his face. "Seems they're all broken up over their friend who took a header off the pier. Don't want to get burned up. Thanks, Suzy Q."

I leaned back in my pseudo-leather chair and sighed. Go ahead, John. Take my suntan lotion. Why not? You've already *borrowed* my tape recorder, my favorite baseball cap, and Lord knows how many pens from me this summer. Oh, yeah. And my dream job. You've likely stolen that from me, too. Bastard.

"Susan." My editor, Frank, leaned out his office. His grizzled beard needed a trim. "Can you come in here a moment, please?"

I grabbed my notepad and hurried in. Maybe he had a big story for me. Maybe I could win this contest after all and get promoted from summer intern to official, full-time reporter.

"I'm awful sorry how this all has turned out," Frank said, his chair squeaking as he settled his large frame into it.

Ugh. Not a good way to start a conversation. I sank into one of the two faded chairs opposite his desk.

"I had high hopes for you at the beginning of the summer," Frank said. "I like your approach to journalism, but these circulation figures don't lie."

He handed me a spreadsheet, pointing to the number at the bottom of column one. Circulation at my weekly paper, *The Cape Times*, which covers the goings on in Cape Ann, New Jersey, was up three percent since I started this internship in May.

"Three percent," I said. "That's really good. Right?"

"Hell, yes. Especially considering how so many papers are going under across the country. Under normal circumstances, I'd be doing a jig, giving you a big kiss, and offering you permanent employment. But these aren't normal circumstances." He poked a stubby finger at the bottom of the next column.

Since the competition began, circulation at *The Bay Banner*, which covers the adjacent town of Atlantic Bay, had risen five percent. Damn! Looked like my nemesis, fellow intern John Bohnert, had the job in the bag.

"He's sure been lucky this summer." My hand flew to my mouth. "Oh, I'm sorry. That's a terrible thing to say."

Frank's eyes twinkled at me. "Don't you worry. You wouldn't be a newspaper reporter at heart if you didn't have a taste for black humor. And John *has* been lucky." He grabbed some old issues of the *Banner* from a teetering pile on his desk. "Five teenagers killed Memorial Day weekend when their car rammed a telephone pole." He pointed at another of John's stories. "Carnival worker died in freak accident while repairing the Ferris wheel."

"It's been like that all summer," I said. "My town's been nice and quiet, while John's town has had one big story after another almost every week."

"And those stories sell newspapers. But don't you feel bad. You've done excellent work." Frank's chair groaned as he leaned back. "Heck, I loved that article about the guy with skin cancer who's using sheep as lawn mowers 'cause his wife won't let him out in the sun anymore. And that interview you did with the high school principal. Ain't she a pistol! Everybody thought they knew her, but who ever would've expected that her favorite vacation spot is her basement?" He chuckled. "You've been reflecting the Cape Ann community, who these folks truly are, in your stories. And they appreciate it. I hear it all the time at the market, at the library, everywhere."

"Any chance Debbie Cheung won't come back from maternity leave?" I asked, hopeful. "John could still win the contest and

get the one open job, but maybe there'll be another opening...
for me?"

Frank smiled. "Nope. Sorry. Debbie's set to start again right
after Labor Day." He clasped his hands over his big belly. "Don't
you worry, Susan. I've got editor friends at every paper in New
Jersey. I'm going to help you find your first permanent job."

I stood. "Thank you. But you know what? There's one more
week left in this contest. I still could outsell John and win the
job. Heck, maybe a serial killer will strike in my town. That
story would sell a ton of copies."

The old newspaper man smiled at me again. "Dare to dream."

* * * *

"I've got it!" Amanda said that night as she slid another bite
of apple pie onto her fork. "We pool all our money together and
buy every copy of *The Cape Times* next week. Circulation will
go up, and you'll land the job."

"Oh, yeah," I said to my roommate as we sat at our battered,
wooden kitchen table. "That'll work. Because we both have
so much spare cash on hand." I'd been earning peanuts at the
newspaper all summer, and Amanda had been selling them—
literally—on the boardwalk, along with every kind of junk food
imaginable, to afford her share of our small, one-story rental.

"Well, there's got to be something we can do. That Bohnert
guy doesn't even like living at the beach, does he?" She cranked
up the volume on her old radio as the Boss began singing "Born
to Run." Gotta appreciate a classic.

I swallowed my Ramen noodles. "No, John's made it very
clear. The only thing he likes about the shore is that it attracts a
lot of girls in the summer." Such a typical guy. "He's aiming for
a big, urban daily. It's completely ironic. All I've ever wanted
was to work at a small newspaper down the shore, settle into a
town, and grow roots. And Cape Ann is perfect. *I* love it here."
I dug in for more noodles. "John sees covering Atlantic Bay as

merely a stepping stone to a more prestigious paper. But he's going to get the job, and I'm going to have to hit my parents up for another loan."

Not that I'm bitter or anything.

"Then tell your editor that." Amanda refilled her water glass at the sink. "The fact that you want the job long term has to count for something, right?"

"You'd think so. But Frank doesn't actually have a say in the matter. This contest was the publisher's idea, and all he cares about is circulation. Frank has to give the one full-time job opening to the intern who increases sales the most this summer. And the folks in Atlantic Bay seem to appreciate John's bad-news approach to journalism more than the Cape Annians like my good-news approach."

Amanda returned to the table and speared another bite of pie. "Want me to rob the convenience store? That'll give you some bad news to cover."

I laughed, my mind going places it shouldn't. "Would you?"

* * * *

"Whoa!" John said over my shoulder a few days later. "Stop the presses!"

I started as John peered at my computer screen. God, I hated how he always snuck up on me like that.

"A record number of adoptions this summer at the animal shelter," he read, smirking. "Hot news, Suzy Q."

I swiveled around in my chair, then stood so we were eye to eye. "Couldn't you once, just once, call me Susan? And it is good news. Don't you like animals?"

"Sure I do. Back at the university, our frat had a dog. You can't imagine the number of chicks I attracted each time I walked that mutt."

How sweet.

"You know, Suzy," he said, while I gritted my teeth at the nickname. "You have to go out and find the big stories. You're never gonna get anywhere in this business if you keep concentrating on all that fluff."

Fluff?! "Let me guess, John. You must be working on a much more important story. Has the pope come to Atlantic Bay and dropped dead? Or maybe you've had a huge bank heist."

"No such luck." He shook his head, looking genuinely disappointed. "But Doug Potter did land in the hospital this morning. I'm just about to write that up."

"Potter?" Frank came out his office. "What happened?"

"Bicycle accident. Broke his left arm and leg and has a concussion," John said.

"Will he be okay?" Frank asked.

"That's what I hear," John said.

"Good." Frank turned to me, apparently taking in the question on my face. "Potter was Atlantic Bay mayor for over a decade in the eighties and nineties. He's one of the most popular mayors the town has ever had."

I sucked in a deep breath. Of course he was.

"In addition to the story on the accident, let's do a sidebar on bicycle safety," Frank said. "And give a call over to Potter's family, John. See if we can get a recent photo."

"Already done," he said. "I'll pick it up before afternoon visiting hours end."

"Great work, John," Frank said. "Really great work."

Yeah. Great. Just great.

* * * *

A couple hours later, I was still tinkering with my animal shelter story when Frank poked his head into the newsroom again.

"Any luck with that Potter photo, John? I bet visiting hours are almost over."

John jumped up, checking his watch. "Shoot. I'll go get it right now." He grabbed his keys and hurried past my desk.

"Hey." Frank called after him. "How's the Potter story coming?"

"Almost done," John said, turning around.

"Don't make it too long. We want to save space for the sidebar."

John nodded. "I'll check back with the family tomorrow morning to get an updated condition that I can plug into the lede. Don't worry. You'll have the story and sidebar by the noon deadline, boss."

"That's perfect," Frank said. "Thanks."

"No problem." John stepped backward toward the door and threw a smirk my way. "Bet this'll sell a whole lot of papers, Suzy Q. A whole bunch."

Both my hands balled into fists. God, I couldn't stand him. I reviewed my animal shelter story one last time and hit send.

The shelter story was a good one. An interesting one. But John had an adored, injured public figure. How could I compete? The *Banner's* circulation would jump again. I could kill John. I really could.

Something quick but painful.

I let out a deep breath and scowled. Time to step up my job hunt.

I went into the back and grabbed an empty cardboard box. In the hopes that this job would become permanent, I'd brought a lot of personal items in during the summer. Better start packing them up.

"Nice work on the shelter story. It only needs a little tightening." Frank approached me a few minutes later while I set some framed photos in the box. "You don't have to take your things home, Susan. Nothing's been decided yet."

"C'mon, Frank. I think the writing's on the wall. Poor Mr. Potter's sealed my fate, hasn't he? John's going to get the job."

"Appears that way. I'm sorry, Susan."

"Me, too. I have one more story for this week's paper, about how the library's patronage is skyrocketing because of the recession. I'll write it up in the morning."

Frank nodded. "When you have a chance, bring me a copy of your resume so I can start calling my pals for you."

He returned to his office. I'd miss working for Frank. He was one of the good guys.

I put my jar of saltwater taffy into the box and took in my nearly bare workspace. Most traces of me from the top of the desk were gone. Only my dog-eared AP Stylebook and the huge Webster's Dictionary I'd bought first year of college remained, along with the standard newsroom equipment: computer, phone, notepads, spiral notebooks, and pens. Shaking off a wave of sadness, I concentrated on what I had left to do. I'd hit the drawers tomorrow.

The police scanner on the counter erupted in chatter. A convenience store robbery. No way! I grabbed my notebook, jotted down the address, and ran to the large map of Cape Ann and Atlantic Bay tacked to the wall. Corner of Ivy and Main streets. Where was it? I scanned the map....Unbelievable. Atlantic Bay. Just over the border from Cape Ann.

Was my town too good for a convenience store robbery? Argh!

The story would be yet another feather for John's cap. At least I already started packing. Hefting the carton onto my right hip, my eyes settled on John's desk against the back wall. My Phillies cap sat on top of a stack of files. Lord, I'd almost forgotten all my stuff he'd *borrowed* this summer. For a guy so particular about nobody touching his computer or messing with his stuff, he had no trouble taking mine.

I carried the box over to John's desk so I could retrieve my belongings. As I set it down, it jostled the computer's mouse, and the screen popped to life. I blinked a few times and shook my head. This didn't make any sense.

"Beloved former Atlantic Bay Mayor Doug Potter, 64, died in his sleep Tuesday night at St. Luke's Hospital, just hours after breaking his left arm and leg in a bicycle accident," I read. *"Potter's death surprised his family, who had been told earlier in the day that he was expected to fully recover.*

"[[Drop in quote from grieving family member.]]," John had written.

The article went on to describe how the doctors didn't know why Potter had taken this turn for the worse, before going into how Potter had lost control of his bicycle on the hilly road by the dunes that he'd biked every morning for years. Then John described Potter's many accomplishments while in office.

I dropped down into John's desk chair. Tuesday night? It was only Tuesday afternoon.

A lump grew in my throat as I remembered those poor high-school kids who died Memorial Day weekend. John had written that story in record time. The police didn't know why their car had veered off the road. The weather was clear. The driver had no drugs or alcohol in his system. Excessive speed wasn't a factor.

And the carnie who died. He'd worked that Ferris wheel for twenty years without incident. That hadn't made sense. And then just last week, that poor girl who somehow slipped off the pier at low tide.

Oh, my God.

I ran to Frank's office. "Is there a way to tell when someone first started writing a story on our network?"

"Umm, yes. I think so. What is it, Susan? You've turned pale."

I swallowed hard, my heart beating wildly. "Frank, I think I might have that serial killer story for you after all."

* * * *

Several hours later, after a whole lot of excitement, I sat in a dim, sticky booth at the only bar near the boardwalk, filling Amanda in.

"You have got to be kidding me," she said, pouring us both another beer from our pitcher.

"Nope. All those accidents this summer—John started writing about each of them before they happened. There's only one way he could've known."

"And the mayor guy?"

"He's okay. The police stationed an officer in the bathroom of Potter's hospital room. When John crept in after visiting hours and started tampering with Potter's IV, the cop jumped him."

Oh, I wish I could've seen that.

Frank approached our table. "Figured I'd find you here." The bags under his eyes had doubled, and his skin seemed ashen. He looked like he'd aged thirty years. "Can I join you?"

"Of course." I introduced him to Amanda.

"Nice to meet you." He squeezed into the booth, his stomach pressing up against the table. "Vodka," he called to the waitress walking by. "And keep 'em coming."

"You can't blame yourself, Frank," I said.

"Can't I? I hired the jerk."

"Why did you hire him?" I asked.

"He's a good writer. He's from Jersey. And he had one fantastic clip from his hometown weekly, where he interned last summer, about a guy who fell in front of a train....Oh. Jesus." Frank downed his drink.

Wow. John really did know how to go out and get the news. Once a psycho, always a psycho.

We all sat quietly for a few minutes, drowning our sorrows. I tried to distract myself, listening to a guy in the next booth hitting on our waitress, who kept shutting him down. No matter what bad things happen, life does go on.

"So you're Susan's roommate?" Frank finally broke the silence, directing his attention to Amanda.

"Yep. I got real lucky," Amanda said. "Susan's neat and quiet. I'll be sorry to see her go at the end of the summer," she said pointedly.

I kicked her under the table. God. Frank would think I asked her to say that.

"I have one more year of school," Amanda went on. "And I'd hoped Susan could stay on in the apartment with me. I love learning about all the news before everyone else does."

"Glad to hear it," Frank said, a smile breaking out on his face. "'Cause I think she'll be sticking around."

Come again?

"At least I hope so." Frank turned to me. "It's such a shame the contest winner is unavailable. I guess the job will have to go to the runner-up." He winked at me. "I spoke to the publisher. The job's yours if you want it."

It took all my strength to act professional and not jump up and down.

"There'll be some big stories to cover, starting in the morning with John's arraignment," Frank said.

I nodded over and over like a fool. "Yes, I want the job. Thank you, Frank, for this opportunity. Thank you!"

Amanda called out for another pitcher of beer. Frank insisted on paying.

Wow. I got the job. And I would cover John's trial. That would be a lot of hard news indeed. I took a large swig from my mug.

Maybe I'd approach John for an interview. Tell him I got the job and for my first story I want to show the world the real him. The man behind the sensation.

Something light. Fluffy.

A real Suzy Q special.

I smiled. It would kill him.

❦

"The Contest" first appeared in the 2010 Deadly Ink Short Story Collection, *published by Deadly Ink Press in 2010.*

Other than writing fiction, I've never had any job I enjoyed more than working as a newspaper reporter. I love small-town news. You can write about weird stuff because it's all about getting to know your neighbors. Indeed, several of the details in this story were based on actual events or people I wrote about over the years. The sheep story, true. The high-school-principal-basement story, true. The serial-killer story? Okay, I made that up. But a girl can dream, can't she? (And in case you think the word lede is misspelled in this story, let me assure you, it's not. It's a term of art in journalism. Hey, just because I write fiction these days doesn't mean I can't include some facts in this book, too.)

THE LORD IS MY SHAMUS

You'd think after all these years, I wouldn't be nervous in his presence. Yet my sandals shook as I approached the swirling cloud.

"You asked to see me?" I crooked my head, trying—but failing—to spot him through the mist. Why was he always such an enigma?

"Yes." His booming voice echoed. "I'm sending you back to Earth to do some investigating for me."

"Investigating?"

"A man has died, and I'd like you to probe those who knew him best. Find out what happened."

Now I know better than anyone that it's not my place to question God. He has his reasons for what he does. But come on. He's omniscient. Why would he need me to investigate anything for him?

"Umm…okay," I said. "But don't you already know what happened?"

He chuckled. "Well, yes, I do. But you of all people understand suffering and the need to know why it happens. So I want you to help this man's family by looking into his death and encouraging the killer to admit his sins and repent."

"The killer? You mean—"

"Yes. This, Job, is murder."

＊ ＊ ＊ ＊

In a blinding flash of light, I found myself in a city. Based on the accents, I figured it was Manhattan—though it could've been Miami or Fort Lauderdale or, really, anywhere in South Florida. I took a moment to take in the sights. Tall buildings. Automobiles zipping by. And the women walking around immodestly in a state of undress. Bare arms and legs and, in a few cases, midriffs. I knew how the Earth had changed during my years in the afterworld—I like keeping up on things—but actually seeing it in person? *Oy vey!*

I glanced down and noticed that my apparel had changed, too. Now I was wearing modern clothes: khaki pants and a pale blue polo shirt. I combed my fingers through my hair. Shorn! My long flowing locks were gone. Cropped to my ears. I raked my fingers over my face and breathed a deep sigh of relief. I'd been allowed to keep my beard, though it apparently had been trimmed and combed. I know I shouldn't care about my appearance, but after you've had the same look as many centuries as I have, you get kind of attached to it.

I turned left from the street corner. The avenue had been busy, but this side street was quieter. Trees and brownstones. A good place to think. My mind drifted back to God. He'd apparently changed my appearance so I'd fit in. And he'd dropped me in the victim's neighborhood, I gathered, so I could get started straight away. But he couldn't be bothered to tell me the killer's name so I could quickly get him to confess and repent? *That* I had to figure out on my own?

I rolled my eyes. (Yes, I'd atone for that later.) Thousands of years had passed, but the Lord still liked to play his little games. I guess when you're all-knowing, yanking my chain helps keep things interesting.

I stepped off the sidewalk, leaned against a nice shady tree, and took a few moments to try to think things through. I had no idea where to go. I patted my pockets. No money. Nowhere to spend the night. I didn't even know the victim's name. *Hey, Lord, how 'bout a little help down here?*

Frustrated, I slapped my hands against my thighs and heard something crinkle. That right pocket had been empty just a moment ago. I reached in and pulled out two scraps of paper. The first one was an obituary for Bruce Goldenblatt, a real-estate investor who had died the previous Saturday, leaving behind a wife and three daughters. The second scrap had an address printed on it—for the brownstone right in front of me.

I glanced up. *Nice aim. And thanks for the assist.*

Time to get down to business. I gazed at the house. Sparkling windows. Spotless front steps bookended by gleaming black wrought-iron railings. Beside the left railing, a handicapped ramp ran from the sidewalk to the stoop. This family might have faced tragedy before. I hoped I could help them now, at least.

It was after the funeral so the family would be sitting *shiva* for seven days, mourning their loved one and focusing on their loss. Who was I to intrude on their grief? While it would be a great *mitzvah* to make a *shiva* call, visitors should be friends and family. I wasn't either. But they'd all be there. An opportunity too good to miss.

I tilted my head, thinking. I could pretend to be an old friend (real old) of Goldenblatt, but they might ask me questions about him that I couldn't answer. I tapped my index finger against my lips. Ah. I'd be a grief counselor, sent over by the rabbi. That should work.

I made my way up the front steps and rang the bell. As I waited, I heard muffled yelling from inside. Soon a girl, maybe fourteen years old with long dark hair, yanked back the door. She was barefoot, wearing a short denim skirt and a low-cut, white tank top, and chewing something pink. Gum, I guessed, though I hadn't seen it firsthand before. Her toenails and fingernails were pink, too. I never would have allowed my daughters to dress that way.

"Hi?" she said. It was a statement, but it came out like a question.

"I don't care!" someone shrieked from behind her. "I don't want children at my wedding."

"How do you expect me not to invite your cousins after they just came to the funeral?" another woman screeched back. "It would be a *shanda!*"

"Too bad!" the first voice screamed. "It's My! Special! Day!"

What was I walking into? "I'm sorry to intrude," I told the girl. "My name is Jo...Joseph." *Close call.* "I'm a grief counselor. Your rabbi suggested I stop by."

The girl turned her head. "Mom! There's some grief counselor here!"

So much yelling. Maybe the family was hard of hearing.

As the girl backed away, a round, middle-aged woman approached the door. Did hair that blond come naturally? She smiled. "Yes?"

"Mrs. Goldenblatt?" She nodded. "Your rabbi sent me over. He thought I might be able to help you during this difficult time." I extended a hand. "I'm Joseph...Bookman. Grief counselor. I'm so sorry for your loss."

"Rabbi Cohen sent you? Well, please come in."

I walked into a small entryway with a glass table in the middle. A large ceramic bowl filled with apples and pears sat on top. To my left was a staircase, straight ahead ran a long hallway with some closed doors lining the left wall, and a large living room was on my right. It had white leather couches, oriental rugs, and glass tables that matched the one in the entryway.

I blinked a couple times, confused. I saw no low stools for mourners to sit on. The mirror on the living-room wall remained uncovered. The woman wasn't even wearing a torn black ribbon in memory of her husband. Except for the fruit bowl in the entryway, which could have been a condolence gift, I saw nothing I'd expect in a home sitting *shiva*. Was I at the correct address?

"It's very nice that Rabbi Cohen has been thinking of us, but really, we're doing just fine," Mrs. Goldenblatt said, motioning me to follow her.

She led me through the house into a shiny chrome kitchen. *Now this was more like it!* Baskets and trays of food covered nearly every available counter, no doubt condolence gifts from friends and family.

The girl who had answered the door trailed behind us, then picked up a mewing gray kitten and climbed onto a bar stool. An older girl sat at a round table staring at a computer screen. An even older girl—a young woman, really—sat at the same table with piles of papers and magazines spread out in front of her. All three girls had the same thin nose, brown eyes, and long dark hair. None of them wore a black ribbon either.

"Girls, this is Mr. Bookman," the mother said. "He's a grief counselor. The rabbi sent him over."

They all looked at me like I'd sprouted another head. I glanced at my shoulders. Nope. No extra head. Thank goodness. That would have been hard to explain, though I'm sure *someone* would have thought it was a riot.

Where to begin? "Again, I'm so sorry for your loss, Mrs. Goldenblatt. And you girls."

"Where are my manners?" the mother said. "Please call me Marjorie. And these are my daughters, Anne, Kayla, and Lauren."

"Stop calling me Kayla," the middle girl said with gritted teeth. "Kay. My name is Kay."

"I'm so sorry, *Kay.*" Marjorie threw her hands in the air. "I did have a role in naming you, you know. Seventeen years you've been Kayla, but noooo. Now suddenly you're Kay."

Oh, yes. A big happy family.

"Kay," I said. "This must be a very hard time for you."

She shrugged. "Yeah. Dad was supposed to take me to look at colleges—I'll start college next fall—but now I have to wait till Mom has time to go. And who knows when that's gonna be. She's completely wrapped up in planning Anne's wedding."

"Lord give me strength," Marjorie said. "I told you I'd find time to take you."

"When?" Kay screeched.

"Soon!" Marjorie yelled back.

This is how they behave with company?

"A wedding," I said to the oldest girl. "How wonderful."

"Yeah, you'd think so," Anne said. "Until your mother starts foisting relatives on you that you don't want to invite." She looked at me with a hopeful smile. "I think the bride should get to choose her own guests, even if she's not paying for the reception. Don't you?"

Oh boy. I didn't want to get into the middle of this. "Well, are they relatives on your father's side of the family? It might be nice to include them, considering his recent passing."

Anne's eyes narrowed, obviously displeased. "Daddy wouldn't have wanted them invited either. He thought our plans were way too expensive. He kept wanting to cut everything down, including the guest list."

"Well, we don't have that problem now, do we?" Marjorie said, striding toward Anne. "Thanks to the life insurance, you can have the big fancy wedding you want. I don't think it's asking very much to invite your cousins! And you!" She turned to Kay. "Stop moping. At least now you can go to any college you want."

She took a deep breath and faced me. "I'm sorry. It's rude of us to talk about money in front of a virtual stranger. It's just been so stressful. Before Bruce died, we'd been having money problems. With the downturn in the economy, Kayla—Kay—was going to have to attend a *state* school, and my Anne would have to have a *scaled-down* wedding. Now Bruce is gone, and so are our money problems. It doesn't seem right."

Indeed. Not right at all. All three of these ladies had a reason to kill.

"What happened to your husband, if I might ask? He was so young," I said.

"He tripped. Fell down the stairs," said a raspy voice behind me. "Broke his neck."

I turned to see an old man with heavy wrinkles around his nose and eyes wheeling himself into the room. He had white hair like mine and a long white beard dotted with crumbs.

I glanced up for a moment. *How come my beard had to be trimmed so much if this guy can wear his beard long?* No response. Figures.

"Dad," Marjorie said. "I'd like you to meet Joseph Bookman. He's a grief counselor. Rabbi Cohen sent him."

"Nice to meet you. I'm Saul," he said as we shook hands. His accent sounded Eastern European. "Terrible thing that's happened. Just terrible."

"Dad witnessed the accident," Marjorie said. "None of the rest of us were home," she added quickly. A bit too quickly, if you ask me.

"What did Mr. Goldenblatt trip on?" I asked Saul.

"My kitten," Lauren, the youngest girl, said, her gaze glued to the feline in her arms. "Squeaker didn't mean to do it!"

"I'm sure she didn't," I said. Especially since I didn't buy the story for a minute.

"Come," Saul said, as he grabbed a pretzel from a bowl on the counter. "I'll show you where it happened."

He wheeled himself toward the front of the house, munching, the wooden floor creaking underneath. "I'm sure the rabbi meant well in sending you over," he said when we were out of earshot of the kitchen. "But I think it's best if the girls don't dwell on this."

He stopped by the front door, clearly wanting me to leave. But I had a job to do.

I turned to the long staircase. "Is this where Mr. Goldenblatt fell?"

"Yeah." Saul rolled up beside me. "The kitten came out of nowhere. Bruce was on his way up, tripped, and fell to the bottom. Poor Lauren's been blaming herself. I really wish she wouldn't."

"It's her cat?" I asked.

"Yep." He nodded. "For good now."

"What do you mean?"

"Lauren only got the kitten a couple months ago. Bruce was terribly allergic. He wanted her to take it back to the pound, but Lauren's attached to Squeaker. She desperately wanted to keep her. Marjorie told Bruce he should keep trying the allergy shots, though to be fair they weren't working." He shrugged. "So now the girl has no father, but she has a cat. Not the best trade off, if you ask me."

Me either. Now all the women in the house had a motive. The yelling in the kitchen resumed, something about chicken or fish. At least they weren't considering pork.

"That must have been a horrible thing to see," I said.

Saul stared at the floor. "Yeah, it was terrible."

Was the old man covering for someone? One of them could have pushed Bruce down the stairs. Did the mother care more about throwing a fancy wedding and sending her daughter to an expensive college than she did about her husband? Or was the bride so selfish that she'd kill her father for the life insurance money? Or her sister with the nickname—was attending some impressive school that important to her? Or the youngest one? Did she choose a kitten over her father?

Sheesh. I'd like to believe none of them was capable of such a horror. Unfortunately I feared otherwise.

"You live here?" I asked Saul.

"Yeah, ever since my Estelle died five years ago." He nodded at a room off the hallway. "Moved in there. It used to be Bruce's home office, but he was nice enough to convert it into a bedroom for me." He rolled closer. "Look, Mr. Bookman, I want you to know, these girls loved their father. And Marjorie loved her husband. I know how it must have sounded back there. So much bickering, especially at a time like this. But that's just their way."

I bent down so Saul and I would be eye to eye, and I laid a hand on his arm. "It must be hard for you, being the only man in the house. Now that Bruce is gone, you're their protector."

He nodded. "Not that I'm really needed. Marjorie's a very strong woman."

"Do you go to *shul*, Saul?" I asked, rising.

"Synagogue? Of course, on the High Holy Days. It's not so easy getting around with this chair, but I manage. We'll all go together next week for *Rosh Hashanah*."

"A time to ask for forgiveness of sins." I began pacing. "There are many sins in this world. It can often seem confusing. If you're trying to help someone you love—to protect them from the consequences of something they've done—is that a sin?"

Saul sat quietly for a moment. "I'd like to think that when God closes the Book of Life each *Yom Kippur*, that he considers everything a person has lived through and everything he's done, not just one act. We all know good men can do bad things."

"And good women."

He stared at me, his lips curling. He wanted to tell me what happened. I could see it.

"Mr. Bookman," he finally said. "I think you should go."

"Go? Already?" Marjorie approached us with a plate of *rugelach*. "You just got here. And I haven't even offered you anything to eat or drink."

I wasn't getting anywhere with Saul. Maybe I could work on Marjorie directly. I turned to her, selected a piece of pastry filled with raisins, and smiled. "A glass of water would be nice. Thank you."

Saul wheeled to his bedroom, muttering to himself, while I followed Marjorie to the kitchen.

* * * *

An hour later, my stomach was stuffed, my head was pounding from all the yelling, and I knew more about the impending wedding than anyone would ever want to know. (Apparently having the same vase and flowers at every table is out. Each table needs its own "pop of style," whatever that means.) But I wasn't any closer to figuring out which of these women needed to unburden herself, and I had the feeling I was wearing out my welcome. I needed to speak to each one alone. But how?

Just then the kitten scampered past. *Ah*. I glanced up. *Thanks*.

"Lauren," I said. "I can tell you feel bad about Squeaker tripping your dad. Why don't we take a little walk and talk about it?"

"Okay," she said and hopped off her barstool.

"I hear your dad was allergic to Squeaker," I said as we entered the hallway, heading toward the front of the house.

She shuffled next to me, focusing on the floor. "Yeah. Anytime Dad was in the same room with Squeaker, his eyes turned red and he started sneezing."

"Must have been hard for you."

"Uh huh." She looked up. "Dad wanted me to give Squeaker back, but Mom convinced him to keep taking the allergy shots. He told me he'd try them for another month, but if things didn't get any better…"

"How'd that make you feel?"

"Mad. I mean I know it wasn't Dad's fault, but why couldn't I have a pet like everyone else?"

I couldn't tell if she was just a typical self-involved teen or something worse. I needed to test her.

"You know," I said as we approached the front staircase, "your grandpa could only see what occurred from a distance. Maybe it just looked like your dad tripped on Squeaker. Maybe he actually tripped on something else. Loose carpeting, perhaps."

Her eyes lit up. "You think?"

She raced to the stairs and scrutinized each one. I followed her up. She looked so hopeful. She really believed it could be true. A good feeling rose in my heart. She couldn't have pushed her father.

When we reached the top, she turned to me, shoulders hunched. "I don't see any loose carpeting. Thanks for trying, Mr. Bookman. I guess Squeaker really is to blame." She burst into tears and ran down the hall. A moment later, a door slammed and loud music began blaring from behind the door.

Great. I made a child cry. More to repent for.

I bent down to examine the top step. Had God sent me on a wild-goose chase? Could Goldenblatt really have just fallen over the cat? Heck, maybe he threw himself down the stairs to get away from all this squabbling. I needed to talk to the other girls to—

I felt hands on my shoulder blades. Then a shove! I began tumbling down the stairs. *Oof! Urk! Hey, my suffering was supposed to be over!*

I landed at the bottom and smacked my brow hard against the entryway table's base. Apples and pears began falling on my head. *Lord, what have I done to deserve this?*

When the pounding stopped, I opened my eyes. Blinked. The room spun. I shut my eyes and waited for someone to come help me up, fearing it could take a while. Between the music upstairs and the yelling from the kitchen, I doubted anyone had heard me fall.

Hey. Wait a minute. Who pushed me?

Not Lauren. I would have seen her coming. Couldn't have been Marjorie. I could clearly hear her in the kitchen. And there was Anne, yelling back, also in the kitchen. And Kay's complaints were wafting down the hallway, too.

What the heck?

The floor creaked, and I felt a shadow fall over me. "God, forgive my terrible temper again," Saul said. "But he was trying to hurt my girls, to blame them for what happened."

Saul?

I opened my eyes. His flew wide.

"You're alive?" he said.

"*You* pushed me?" I said, eyeing his wheelchair. "And Bruce? But how?"

He suddenly appeared very old and scared. "The elevator." He nodded toward one of the closed doors in the hall. "Bruce had it installed for me when I moved in."

An elevator in a house? I guess I wasn't as up on the modern world as I'd thought.

"I don't understand," I said, trying to get up but slumping back down. *Oy*, my head hurt. "He let you move into his home. Gave you his office. Enabled you to get around the whole house, apparently. Why would you do this to him, Saul?"

He paused. For a moment he seemed far away, lost in thought. Then he held out his left forearm and pushed up the sleeve. Tattooed numbers. I sighed deeply.

"I was a teenager when we were sent to the camps," he said. "Auschwitz. I never saw my mother and sisters again." He shivered and shook his head, as if he could make the memories disappear. "I was the only member of my family to survive. When the war ended, I promised myself I'd create a new family and I'd protect them from everything."

"But Bruce loved you and the girls. Didn't he? How was he a threat?"

Saul gazed toward the kitchen, where the argument had moved on to the flavor of the wedding cake. "Marjorie and the girls raise their voices, but not Bruce. Never Bruce. Until the economy turned, and he lost a lot of money in the market." Saul wrung his hands. "He wanted Marjorie and the girls to sacrifice. A small wedding. A state school. That I could understand, but he had no right to yell at my Marjorie."

He paused. I stared quietly at him, hoping my silence would encourage him to continue. Finally, he did.

"The day Bruce died," Saul said, "he and Marjorie had another argument about money, much louder than the one going on right now. He called her extravagant, said she was spoiling the girls. Marjorie called him a tightwad and insisted on her way, but Bruce said that for once he was going to get his way. Marjorie's waterworks wouldn't work. Marjorie stormed out, and Bruce headed up the stairs here. I was at the top, where I'd been listening. I couldn't help myself. I was so angry. My Marjorie deserved to be treated like a queen! You don't scream at queens." Tears spilled from his eyes. "No one suspected a thing. Just like they won't with you."

He grabbed the ceramic fruit bowl and raised it over my head.

"Daddy, no!" Marjorie ran toward us. "Not again!"

Saul's arms quivered as he lowered the bowl. I let out a deep breath. I'd died once before. Believe me, once had been enough.

Marjorie grabbed the bowl from Saul's outstretched hands and clutched it to her chest.

"You know?" he asked her.

A tear ran down her cheek. "I thought you did it for the money, Daddy. So Anne could have her wedding and Kayla could go to a good school. I didn't know you killed Bruce because of me. You shouldn't have. I loved him. He was a good man."

Saul leaned back in the chair, his face ashen. "It was the yelling, Marjorie. I couldn't stand that he yelled at you."

"I'm a grown woman, Daddy. I could have handled it."

"I know," he said quietly. "I lost my temper. I'm sorry."

While they were talking, I'd struggled to my feet. My head hurt, but I'd felt worse. Marjorie seemed to notice me at that moment.

"Oh, Mr. Bookman. Please don't turn my father in. He did a terrible thing, but his heart was in the right place. He's suffered so much already, and we need him here with us."

I looked at her and then at Saul for a good while, and I understood why God had sent me.

"You should go to your rabbi, both of you. Confess what happened. He'll help you find your way."

Marjorie's eyes widened, afraid, but Saul nodded.

"You're right, Bookman. I'll go. We'll both go." He held out his hand, and I shook it. "It'll be good getting it all off my chest. Maybe we can find a way to let Lauren know that she wasn't to blame because of her cat. And I'm sorry about...this." He gestured at the bowl and had the decency to look sheepish.

I nodded and turned back to Marjorie. "I have to ask. You said you weren't home at the time. How did you know what happened?"

"Yeah," Saul said. "How?"

She set the bowl on the table. "I was only gone a couple minutes, Daddy. Remember? Got as far as the corner, then turned around. I came in, saw Bruce, and screamed. You called from upstairs that you were on the phone with 911. You said Bruce had tripped over Squeaker halfway up the stairs. Fell all the way down."

"So?" Saul asked.

"I knew Bruce couldn't have tripped over Squeaker. Bruce would have known if Squeaker were anywhere near him. He started sneezing whenever the cat came within five feet." She sniffed hard and reached out, plucking a large crumb from Saul's beard. "And then I saw some pretzel crumbs on Bruce. You're the only one of us who eats pretzels, Daddy. You eat them constantly, as if you're afraid we'll run out of food. I knew Bruce must have made it to the top of the stairs, and you must have touched him. It's the only way crumbs from your beard would have fallen onto him. So I knew you lied about how he fell."

Saul turned my way, looking surprised yet also proud. "That's my girl," he said. "A regular Columbo."

* * * *

I said my goodbyes, left the brownstone, and by the time I reached the sidewalk, *poof!* I was home again. My hair was long, and I had on my favorite robe and sandals.

The swirling cloud appeared before me. "A job well done, Job."

"So it was Saul, huh?" I said. "I didn't suspect him for a minute. I knew all about elevators, but I didn't know they put them in houses. That's what I get for taking classes from Moses. Sure, he knows his *Torah*, but he also got lost in the desert for forty years. I never should've expected he'd get all the details on the modern world right."

God chuckled.

"I hope I handled things the way you wanted," I said.

"Yes. You got Saul to confess his sin and Marjorie to admit she knew about it. Good work."

"Too bad I nearly had to die to do it," I said.

"Well," God said, "it's not like you haven't died before."

Easy for you to say.

"If there's nothing else," I said, "I think there's a pinochle game going on."

The mist began swirling more.

"I'll speak to you again soon, Job." If a cloud could wink, I'd swear this one did. "Hopefully things won't be so dangerous the next time."

Next time?!

❀

"The Lord Is My Shamus" originally appeared in Chesapeake Crimes: This Job Is Murder, *published by Wildside Press in 2012. This story was nominated for the 2012 Agatha Award.*

One thing mystery authors (perhaps all authors) often try to do is come up with an idea for an original protagonist. I'm no different, but it's not so easy. Until one day I had a eureka moment. Who'd be more original than

God? I hadn't recalled him starring in any amateur-sleuth series. Of course, there's probably a reason for that. If God is omniscient, then he already knows who did it, which would take the fun, and the mystery, out of the story. So I stored God away in the back of my mind, until I was trying to come up with a story idea for Chesapeake Crimes: This Job Is Murder. *I saw the word "job," which was intended to mean something you do for money, and I thought "Job," the tortured biblical character. What if God sent Job back to Earth to do some investigating for him and try to right some wrongs? And if Job happened to suffer some more while he was at it, well, would that be so bad? I shared the idea with a friend, who laughed with delight. A job for Job. Yes, I knew I had something there.*

BISCUITS, CARATS, AND GRAVY

We have three big Thanksgiving traditions in my family. Everyone gathers at my house. We all hold hands when we give thanks. And we all avoid my big sister Agnes's gravy like the plague.

Unfortunately, I can never dodge it entirely.

"Happy Thanksgiving, Dotty," Agnes said, click-clacking into my kitchen, holding out her gravy container as if it held gold. More like mold, if this year's version resembled last year's. And every year's before that.

"Happy Thanksgiving, Agnes." I pecked her on the cheek as she handed off her creation. I set it down next to my silver gravy boat. My poor boat that everyone passed around the table each year, never actually pouring anything from it. Not that you could. Agnes used so much flour, the gravy practically stood up on its own.

"You want me to use the lower oven again this year, Dotty?" asked my brother-in-law, Fred, carrying in Agnes's turkey.

Someone should have told that man years ago that just because it's Thanksgiving, he doesn't have to wear a bright orange sweater with a turkey on it. Nonetheless the same sweater. Every year.

"Sure do," I said. "It's already set to keep the bird warm until we sit down to eat."

Agnes and I divvy up the cooking each Thanksgiving. Since I host, she takes on the turkey and gravy. I handle everything else. Agnes and Fred live only a few blocks away, so splitting things is easy. Quite frankly, I'd rather be in charge of the turkey and gravy, too. It's such a shame that every year the family gets a mostly perfect meal. But I haven't been able to figure out a kind way to keep Agnes out of the kitchen. Not yet anyway.

I heard the front door open and close again, and I stepped into the foyer. Almost the whole clan had arrived: both my girls, their husbands, and kids; my son, Michael, with his wife, Charlene, and kids; and most of the brood from Agnes's side.

As I hugged everyone hello, I scanned my living room one more time. The maroon couch pillows were plumped and set at exactly the right angles. That tiny spot that had somehow appeared this morning on my beautiful white carpeting had been exorcized. Nice classical music provided a peaceful yet sophisticated background. And both the cornucopia on the coffee table and the pumpkin-scented candles atop the accent tables provided the perfect finishing touches.

Martha Stewart, eat your heart out.

If only things could stay like this. I tried to ignore my six-year-old grandson, Bobby, who was sitting on the arm of one of the wing chairs. The arm! Just then I noticed my granddaughter Libby had set her glass on a table without a coaster. The girl is thirteen years old. She should know better. I shot her a look. She fixed things right quick. My stars, this younger generation has no sense of propriety.

Agnes stepped into my dining room. I followed, feeling calmer. I knew this room would still be perfect, still undisturbed by others' hands. And it was. The linen napkins were properly positioned and folded. The Waterford glasses and wine goblets were set at the correct angle to the plates. Both my china and the mahogany table underneath it shone in the light reflecting off my crystal chandelier. I sighed with happiness.

"Everything looks exceptional, Dotty, as always," Agnes said.

"Thanks." I nodded my head. Couldn't help smiling. Yes, everything appeared just right.

Michael had put all three leaves into the table this morning so we could fit all twenty-four of us around it. I was pleased, even though it was going to be a pretty tight squeeze. Tight enough that my husband, Henry, sitting at the far end, wouldn't have much room to scooch his chair back to unbutton his pants as the meal progressed. That, of course, was a plus.

I felt a tug on my arm.

"Grandmother, come see!" Bobby pulled me toward the front door. My daughter-in-law, Charlene, was taping up a sign that declared "Happy Thanksgiving" in orange and blue crayon. Beside the words was a picture of a...

"Is that a dog?" I asked, tilting my head, trying to decipher the drawing. It kind of resembled a cow crossed with a giraffe, but I guessed dog based on the long ears and tail and brown coloring.

"Yes," Charlene said, beaming at Bobby. "He made this for you this morning. He can't draw a turkey yet."

I laughed. Good heavens. Claude Monet he wasn't. But at least Bobby spelled the words correctly. And his heart was in the right place.

I leaned down and gave him a hug. "Thank you."

"You're welcome." He looked slyly at his mother then back at me. "Maybe for Christmas you could give me a dog?"

I laughed some more while Charlene's face turned red. Boy, did she have her hands full with this one. He was crafty. Had to appreciate that.

"You'll have to talk to your mother about that," I said.

One of my timers dinged, and I hurried off to pull a pan of biscuits from the oven while I heard Bobby say, "Can I, Mama? Please?"

A dog. Dear Lord. I shivered, thinking of the potential mess.

I'd barely set foot into my quiet kitchen before Agnes was hot on my heels. "Did you remember to set a place for Jessica?" she asked.

"Of course." How could anyone forget the bottle-blond bimbo dating Kevin, her oldest grandchild? Last year at Thanksgiving, Jessica wore such a low-cut, tight sweater I swear Henry nearly mentioned it when he shared what he was thankful for. "It's going to be a tight fit in there. Any more grandchildren, and we'll have to think about setting up a children's table, like Mother and Daddy used to do."

"Who knows, maybe next year there'll be great-grandchildren on the way," Agnes said with a lilt in her voice.

I stopped short, nearly dropping the biscuits.

"Kevin has asked Jessica to marry him!" Agnes said.

Dear Lord have mercy. I was going to have to smile at that girl across my Thanksgiving table for the rest of my life. If only she didn't always have such a vacant look in her eyes. Or could spell vacant.

"What wonderful news," I said. "When did this happen?"

"Just last night. Don't say anything. They're planning to announce it during dinner. I promised Kevin he could have Mother's engagement ring." She fluttered her right hand. "I'm going to give it to him when they make the announcement, so he can put it on Jessica's finger while the whole family watches."

Mother's engagement ring? She was going to give Mother's two-carat, platinum-set, colorless engagement ring to that twenty-year-old, gold-digging airhead? I took a few quick breaths. I hadn't minded when Mother left her stunning diamond ring to Agnes when she passed a few years ago. We split up the family heirlooms fairly evenly. And the oval-shaped ring looked so nice on Agnes. She had thinner fingers than Mother had, so the ring accentuated Agnes's long, lean hands. She wore the ring on the index finger of her right hand, keeping Mother closer to her heart, according to a Jewish tradition Agnes had learned about on some cable show. I thought that was a nice sentiment, so I truly had no problem with Agnes getting Mother's ring— until now. I'd simply never dreamed Agnes would let the ring out of the family. It should be going to a granddaughter, not a granddaughter-in-law!

"Well, isn't that lovely," I said, trying to keep my voice chipper and steady while I avoided Agnes's gaze. It wouldn't do to express my concern. Certain people would think I was jealous, when, really, I only wanted things kept proper.

I set the biscuits down on the kitchen table and examined everything on it, trying to find something to focus on instead of Agnes. I needed a distraction. The sweet potato salad looked good after chilling overnight. Next to it sat two cans—*cans!*— of cranberry sauce. In my house! They must be the work of my eager-beaver daughter-in-law. Charlene always meant well, but her taste certainly left something to be desired. As did her hair style. I shuddered, moving my eyes along. When I spotted my gravy boat, I had an idea. A wonderfully delicious idea.

"Agnes, give me the ring," I said, turning toward her. "Let me shine it. It's a little dull now. It should be perfect when Kevin gives it to Jessica."

She smiled at me. "Oh, Dotty, you're always so thoughtful."

Yes. I smiled back. I was.

* * * *

About an hour later, we all sat around the dining-room table, hands clasped, sharing thanks. It was an enlightening experience, to say the least. Apparently my eleven-year-old granddaughter, Ellie, is most thankful for some singer named after carpeting. Justin Berber or something like that. I hoped I might get a more thoughtful answer from my fifteen-year-old grandson, Tim, but no. He's most thankful for the success of the Carolina Panthers this season. Henry wasn't much better. His lips said he's thankful for his family, but his eyes roamed to a sweater he shouldn't have been noticing.

Yes, Kevin and the airhead had shown up. With her breasts practically sitting on the table, she mooned at Kevin and said she was thankful for him. Nothing else. Solely him. And my idiot grand-nephew ate it up. Maybe she did love him. I hoped so. But I feared she loved our money more.

Finally we made it to Agnes, who sat to my left. She always liked giving her thanks last.

"I'm so thankful that our entire family still lives right here in Fayetteville and that we're all close," she said. "With the turmoil you see in the news every day, we're so lucky to have been blessed with health and prosperity. I'm thankful to the Goodyear company for promoting Floyd and Charles again this year." She beamed at both her sons, who are in management at the tire manufacturer.

"I'm thankful for Fred and Margaret and..." Agnes went on as she always does, naming every single member of the family. "And, finally, I'm thankful for my little sister, Dotty, who takes on the responsibility for this meal every year and who has been my best friend my whole life."

Now she smiled at me. I took the opportunity to squeeze her hand and get a better grasp on Mother's engagement ring.

"Agnes, you are so sweet, as always." I slid my hand away, easily pulling the ring with me, thanks to the butter I had rubbed on the inside of the band after I shined it. "Henry, I think it's time."

All eyes shifted to the other end of the long table where my husband rubbed his palms together, relishing the imminent delight of carving the bird. He loved it so much you'd think he was a butcher in a prior life. Or a mass murderer. I took that opportunity to stretch my arm out over the gravy boat and drop Mother's ring in it. The ring sank with nary a ripple.

I hated having to hide the ring in the gravy. Lord knows what might grow on it until I got the chance to fish it out, but it was the best spot. No one would find it in there. And I just had to keep it safe until Libby got married. After all, as the oldest female grandchild, the ring was rightly hers. When the time came, I'd simply find the ring under the credenza or behind the sideboard or something like that. I could explain it away.

About fifteen minutes later, after we all had finished our soup, and slices of turkey had begun making their way around the table, along with my mashed potatoes, green-bean casserole, and homemade cranberry sauce (so there, Charlene!), Agnes gasped.

"Mother's ring!" she said. Well, screamed is more like it. My sister may be in her seventies, but she has the lungs of a choir girl. "It's gone!"

"What do you mean, it's gone?" Jessica screeched.

It was the first interaction she'd had with anyone but Kevin since she walked in the door. Yep, just what I thought. She wanted Kevin for the family money.

"Now, now, dear, I'm sure it's here somewhere," my brother-in-law, Fred, said to Agnes. "Didn't you take it off earlier?"

Agnes rolled her eyes at him. "Yes, I took it off so Dotty could polish it. But she returned it to me, and I put it back on. I specifically remember that."

"Well, where did that happen?" he asked.

"In the kitchen, while we were…" Agnes stopped talking. Her mouth fell open. "Oh, no."

Oh, no, what?

"What's the matter, Grandmother?" Kevin asked.

"I slipped the ring on while we were putting the final touches on everything," Agnes said, waving her arm at the table. "All the food."

I never knew silverware could make such noise. It clattered as everyone dropped their utensils. A couple of forks fell to the floor. Dang it. I'd have to get the steam cleaner out after dinner.

I put a calming hand on Agnes's shoulder. "Don't worry. I'm sure we'll find it when we clean up. Now everybody eat up before the food gets cold."

"Eat up?" Jessica said. "Are you crazy? Someone could swallow my ring!"

"*Your* ring?" Charlene and both my daughters echoed in unison.

"Yes. Kevin and I are getting engaged. He's supposed to give me the ring tonight. It was gonna be a big surprise." She glared at Kevin as if this were all his fault. "Do something!"

The boy looked bewildered. "Like what?"

"Like what?" Jessica said. "How 'bout like this?!" And she jammed her hands deep into the bowl of cranberry sauce sitting in front of her. The juice sloshed over the side, right onto my gleaming table. Jessica kept wiggling her hands, making a bigger and bigger mess.

Everyone sat staring at her. Finally Jessica pulled her hands from the cranberries, the sauce dripping down her arms. "It's not in there!" With frantic eyes and literally heaving breasts, she then thrust her hands into the bowl of brussels sprouts, causing some of them to catapult out of the bowl, across the room. "Help me!" she screamed.

And Lord have mercy, everyone did. Before I could stop it, Kevin was destroying the green-bean casserole, running his hands all through it while chunks flew out—some landing in his hair. My granddaughter Ellie and grand-niece Cheryl flapped their hands through the mashed potatoes. Fred grabbed the remains of the turkey carcass and shoved his arm inside, feeling it up.

"No ring," he called. "Just stuffing!"

Then the rest of the grandchildren got into the mix, and in moments, broccoli and honey-glazed carrots were flying through the air, hitting the walls and other members of the family.

I thought I was going to have a heart attack. Right then and there.

I stared at Henry, my hand on my chest. "Help!"

You would think that after being married to me for nearly fifty years, the man would know what I meant. That he had to stop the madness. But nooo. He joined in! He shoved his hands into my exquisite endive salad with candied pecans. Soon greens and nuts and blue-cheese dressing were soaring this way and that. And once my husband had joined in, everybody else apparently thought it was the right thing to do, too.

My older daughter slung her arm into the bowl of roasted butternut squash and parsnip soup sitting on the sideboard. Waves rolled over the side of the bowl, splashing onto the table and floor. My younger daughter dragged the scalloped sweet potatoes to her and began pulling the dish apart, bit by bit. Everywhere people were yelling about their lack of success while food was being flung about and Jessica kept shouting orders to keep looking. You couldn't have screamed "food fight" and gotten a bigger mess.

I leaned back in my chair, breathing heavily, watching my perfect Thanksgiving dinner descend into chaos.

Even Agnes was searching the food on her plate and mine. I quickly grabbed the gravy boat and pulled it toward me, trying to shield it from the fray.

Jessica looked frantic. "Get the desserts!" she ordered, and Kevin and his brothers ran into the kitchen. In moments my peach cobbler, pumpkin pie, and apple pie made it to the table, where they all were ravaged one by one. "Where is it?" Jessica screamed. "We have to find it!"

By that point, my youngest grandsons apparently thought this was their one and only chance to make a mess at their grandmother's house. They started throwing the biscuits at each other. One hit a glass of red wine, which sloshed down the front of Charlene's dress. Another soared over my head and hit the oil painting of my grandfather on the wall. I hurried to straighten it—he was an Army man and would be rolling over in his grave if he saw this bedlam. When I turned back, I watched, seemingly in slow motion, as another biscuit flew toward me. Fast and low. Near the tabletop. And then it hit the gravy boat dead on. The boat tipped, and I froze as the thick, brown gravy began oozing out, onto the table, over the edge, and onto my luxurious white carpeting.

It would never come out.

For a few seconds, I couldn't hear anything but my own heart booming erratically in my chest. A feeling of light-headedness came over me. Lord, just take me now, I thought. This would never happen to Martha Stewart.

Then I swallowed hard and forced myself to my senses. The ring hadn't slid out of the boat. I could buy new carpeting. All wasn't lost. Not yet anyway.

I jumped forward, quickly righted the gravy boat, and glanced around to see if I could snag the ring without anyone noticing. Everyone remained focused on creating their own mess. Everyone but Jessica, who had moved much closer and stood staring at me, a glint in her definitely not-vacant eyes, as she held the basket of biscuits in one hand and my mud cake with white chocolate ganache in the other. She wasn't even bothering to search the cake. She was wobbling it in her hand, letting me know plain and clear that the choice of whether the cake met my carpeting was all up to me.

"I so hope we find the ring, Aunt Dotty," she said, her voice calm and cold. "If it's not in the food, it must be somewhere hidden in the house. I'd hate to have to call the sheriff and report that it's apparently been stolen by someone in the family. Larceny at Thanksgiving. How could your family ever live down the shame?"

My eyes betrayed me, growing wide.

She knew.

"And then I'm sure the newspaper would show up," Jessica said. "And they'd take pictures of all of this." She cast her arms wide, the cake tipping precariously. "What would all your neighbors say at church on Sunday?"

I took in the room again. Scalloped sweet potatoes and cranberry sauce dotted the walls, like one of those abstract paintings where the so-called artists flick paint at the canvas. Several glasses of pinot noir lay on their sides, the wine dripping off the table. The turkey looked as if it had been attacked by vultures. Food was plastered into the children's hair and onto everyone's clothes. Everywhere I looked there was mess.

No. Not just mess. Disaster.

I turned my attention back toward Jessica, licked my lips, and sighed. The airhead had beaten me.

"Oh, my," I said. "Here it is!"

I reached down into the gravy boat and plucked out the ring. As I held it up, Jessica smirked, and silence descended in the room.

"You found it," Kevin said.

"Thank goodness," Agnes added.

"Oh," Jessica said. "I'm so relieved!"

As she said it, she whirled sideways, and the mud cake flew from her hand, hitting me square in the nose and forehead. Gooey bits clung to my eyelashes. Then the cake began to slowly slide down my face and clothes before ultimately landing at my feet. My humiliation was complete.

"Oh, Aunt Dotty. I'm so sorry," Jessica said. "I don't know how that happened." Jessica stepped forward into the cake, squishing it into the carpet. As I tried to brush the cake from my eyelids, Jessica pulled the ring from my hand and held it up for all to see. "But at least we've recovered the ring."

It was at that moment that Agnes seemed to really notice the state of my dining room. "Oh, Dotty, I'm sorry, too. Your beautiful furniture and carpeting. They're ruined. And your walls. You'll have to repaint." She grabbed one of my white linen napkins and handed it to me so I could start wiping the chocolate off my face and dress. "It's all my fault. I should have been more careful when I helped you set up." She paused, blinking. "But it's funny, I don't even remember going near the gravy boat after you filled it."

I nodded. Bits of cake fell from my hair. "Don't you worry about this at all, Agnes. It's not your fault."

"That's right," Jessica said. "I'm sure if *you* had noticed the ring falling into the gravy, Grandmother Agnes, you would have said something right away. You never would have wanted to have this pristine room ruined while we searched for the ring. Isn't that right, Aunt Dotty?"

I nodded again and nearly laughed aloud over the absurdity of the situation.

Maybe it wouldn't be so bad having this girl in the family. She wasn't such a dim bulb after all.

"Agnes," I said as I licked some of the cake crumbs from my lips. "I think starting next year we should change some of our family traditions. Let's have Thanksgiving dinner at your house. You can take care of the jobs of hosting and cooking all the side dishes. I'll just make the turkey."

"And I'll make the gravy," Jessica said, grinning at me for real. "The meal just wouldn't be the same without it."

❦

"Biscuits, Carats, and Gravy" originally appeared in The Killer Wore Cranberry, *published by Untreed Reads Publishing in 2010.*

When Editor-In-Chief Jay Hartman of Untreed Reads Publishing put out a call for stories for his first Thanksgiving anthology, he said he wanted funny Thanksgiving crime stories, each featuring a holiday food. He would be choosing one story for each type of dish. My mind started working overtime. Funny. Hmm. It would be hard to make murder funny. Maybe I could use another crime, such as theft. I figured Jay would get a slew of submissions featuring the Thanksgiving biggies:

*turkey, pumpkin pie, and green-bean casserole, and that
my chances of acceptance would be higher using a dish
other authors might overlook. Like gravy. And the ideas
rolled out from there. Could something small be stolen
and hidden in gravy? Oh, yes. Could a family end up
searching through their meal for missing jewelry? Uh
huh. Could that search believably boil down to a food
fight? Yep, yep it could. I had such fun writing this story.
I hope you enjoyed reading it.*

CHRISTMAS SURPRISE

Eyes on the prize, Rob. Keep your eyes on the prize.

I kept repeating the words to myself. Maybe if I thought them often enough, I wouldn't strangle the perky secretary who'd offered me a cup of eggnog—twice—in the past five minutes while I waited for my appointment.

"It shouldn't be much longer," she said, her baby blues twinkling behind the granny glasses perched on the tip of her nose. "It's wonderful you've returned home, Robbie."

I grinned at her, growling inside. I didn't know what pissed me off more, that she called me Robbie, as if I were six, or that I was actually home.

Home. The day I turned eighteen, I'd fled the North Pole and its damned cheerfulness. Vowed never to return. Yet here I was, ten years later, sitting in the human resources office of Santa's workshop, hoping to land a job. At least they had the heat cranked up. I'd forgotten how the Arctic cold seeped into my bones. If I were in charge, I'd move the whole operation down to the tropics. Nothing beat being warm.

Finally bells jingled as Andy, the head elf, opened his office door. He wore a belted, long green shirt and a freaking cone-shaped green hat with a white pompon on the end. And tights! Jesus, I hated everything about this place, especially all the ridiculous clothes everyone wore. Why couldn't they just wear jeans?

I approached Andy, my hand outstretched. He ignored it, enveloping me in a bear hug. I had to force myself not to squirm. Everyone around here was way too touchy-feely.

"Robbie, it's great to see you," he said.

"Thanks. You, too." Nothing like starting a job interview with a lie.

"Well, come on in," he said. "It's certainly been a long time."

We entered Andy's office. It smelled of cinnamon. Large, framed photos of the boss and his wife, white-haired and apple-cheeked, hung on the far wall. Andy had always been such a suck-up. His desk was littered with small toys. A yo-yo, stuffed brown bear, and a red race car, among others. He caught me eyeing them as he settled behind his desk.

"Prototypes," he said. "We're trying to take classic toys and update them for the twenty-first century. It's a challenge." A large smile spread over his face. "But we love a challenge up here."

I sank into the chair in front of his desk, trying like hell not to retch all over his prototypes, which still looked retro to me. I nodded, my mouth shut tight, so I wouldn't say something inappropriate.

"So," Andy said. "Not too many elves ever leave Christmas Town. How'd the big world treat you?"

Just great, until I pulled that five-year stretch in the joint. You haven't really done prison time till you've done it as an elf.

I'd keep that thought to myself. This wasn't the time for honesty.

"Dandy," I said instead. I knew this guy would never check. Everyone up here was so trusting. That stuff about Santa knowing when kids are good or bad? Don't believe it for a second. The sap likes to think that everyone is always good.

Andy flashed an even bigger smile now. I wanted to smack it off his face, but I smiled back at him instead. Had to put on a good show.

"Glad to hear it," he said. "So what brings you back here?"

If I said revenge, he'd never hire me. But that was the reason. My need for revenge consumed me. I used to lie awake at night in that bitter, reeking prison, dreaming of getting out and tracking down my old squeeze, Lisa. I'd thought she'd been cool with my little side business when she discovered it. What's a little burglary between friends? Then she ratted me out to the cops. I spent five years in that freezing hellhole because of her. Five years of watching my back—often unsuccessfully. The guys loved using me as a punching bag. And more. Oh, Lisa had to pay.

She must have known I'd eventually come looking for her, because when they finally sprung me, Lisa had vanished. Couldn't get a lead on her anywhere. But there was one guy who could find her: Santa. So here I was, sucking down the bile in my throat while I sucked up to Andy.

"I missed home, all the other elves, the caroling, everything," I said, trying to keep my voice light and peppy. "So I've moved back and am looking for a job. Can you help me?"

"Of course." Andy leaned forward. "There's always room for another elf in Santa's workshop, especially with Christmas just two months away. What department did you have in mind?"

"Dolls. I want to make dolls."

"Easy enough. Lots of little girls want dolls."

I smiled. I was counting on it.

* * * *

A couple months later, I'd constructed an army of dolls. They sang. Laughed. Talked baby talk. The works. It took all my self-control not to snap their little heads off.

I'd also created one special doll. It didn't walk or talk or do anything. Just waited for a kid with imagination to give it life. I named it Amy, after Lisa's daughter. It was exactly the kind of toy a kid raised by goody-two-shoes Lisa would want. The girl was a toddler when I went inside. She'd be the perfect age for this doll now.

I entered my doll into the database and pressed search. Seconds later I got the response I'd hoped for. Amy the doll and Amy the kid were a match. I couldn't help laughing. Just a few days till Christmas. Oh, payback would be sweet.

* * * *

Finally Christmas Eve arrived. The reindeer were warmed up and harnessed. Santa was doing his last-minute prep, tucking his PDA in his left pocket while the missus stuffed candy—bars and canes—in his right. I was part of the team making sure the toys were strapped in properly. Davey, one of the shortest elves, kept singing that obnoxious "We Are Santa's Elves" song. Jeez, I so needed to get out of here.

Once the toys were secured, I hung back as the other elves headed to the bar for some eggnog and more—*more!*—caroling. I made sure no one was looking and hid in the back of the sleigh, behind the toys. A few minutes and some ho-ho-ho's later, Santa and I were on our way.

I'd never ridden in the sleigh before. It was frigging cold up there in the atmosphere. No wonder Santa always wore that furry suit. I couldn't wait till we got to Lisa's place. I needed a little warmth, and oh, I was gonna get it from her.

Each time we stopped, my nerves jangled in anticipation. Was this the house? I kept waiting for the Amy doll to float out of the sleigh and land in Santa's sack—my personal signal that we'd reached Lisa's place. (What, you thought flying reindeer were the only magical thing about Christmas?)

Several hours into the trip, somewhere on the U.S. East Coast, we reached my destination. A small ranch house with blinking, colored lights lining the roof and a lopsided snowman partially melted in the yard. I watched Santa, the Amy doll, and a few other toys drop down the chimney. My adrenaline flowing, I crawled out of the sleigh, crept past the reindeer, and squatted on the far side of the chimney. Before I knew it, Santa was up and out, back in the sleigh, and off to deliver the rest of his gifts.

And I was finally in a position to deliver mine.

I grasped the chimney, swung my legs inside, and began climbing down. Bricks scratched my back and palms, but I couldn't stop thinking about my plans for Lisa. I'd sneak into her bedroom and—*what the hell?* I'd almost reached the bottom of the chimney, but I was stuck.

I wiggled around. Soot fell on my face. I coughed and shook some of it off, but couldn't move up or down. How had the damn chimney suddenly become so narrow? No way that lardo Santa could make it down and I couldn't.

And then I remembered: Christmas magic. I'd never paid much attention in elf school. I'd known I'd be ditching Christmas Town first chance I got, so I'd figured I didn't need to know all the crap they taught. But I vaguely recalled something about Christmas magic. It's how Santa fits into chimneys. They expand for him. And only him. Son of a bitch! What was I gonna do?

I had no choice. I needed help.

"Lisa," I yelled. No answer. "Lisa!"

I heard scurrying below.

"Mommy, it's Santa!"

"Oh, my God," Lisa said.

She sounded squeaky, like she had in court, when she'd testified against me. She knew who was up the chimney, and she was scared. Good.

"You better go right back to bed, Amy," Lisa said. "You don't want Santa to catch you awake. Make sure you shut your door and stay in bed until morning."

I heard the girl giggle, then sounds of retreating footsteps. A few moments later a door slammed.

"Rob, is it really you?" Lisa's voice trembled.

"Yeah, baby. I'm your Christmas surprise," I said, low and smooth. Lisa would help me out of this jam—she was such a Girl Scout—but it couldn't hurt to turn on the charm. "I'm stuck. You need to pull me down."

"How did you find me?"

I bit back a curse. Nothing was ever simple with this woman. "I've missed you, baby. Waited so long to surprise you. Does it really matter how I tracked you down?"

"No. I guess it doesn't....You're really stuck in there?"

"Yeah." Christ. Why would I lie about that?

"Okay, give me a minute to figure out what to do."

Dumb bitch. I'd told her what to do. Yank me out. At least I was far enough down the chimney that I was starting to warm up. Then I heard a popping sound. And another. What was that?

"I like to think of myself as a good person, but I don't see any other option," Lisa said as the crackling grew louder. "I tried to hide from you, Rob, but obviously Amy and I will never be safe, not as long as you're alive."

It was at that moment that my feet started to sweat and smoke curled into my nostrils. And I knew.

She'd lit the Yule log. And I was toast.

※

This is another story that came to me, practically fully formed, in a dream. I enjoyed adding color to it, giving nods to the wonderful holiday TV specials from my childhood through the elves' clothing and carols. Of course, those shows always had happy endings. Ah, well...

One of the joys of being a writer is being able to say thank you to friends through my writing. I have several former colleagues who have long supported me, always asking about my work. I hope to eventually name story characters after all of them, in appreciation. In this story, I've singled out four: Rob Garrett, Dave Holloway, Lisa Kimmel, and Amy Hallett. I hope you like your namesakes.

SUFFER THE LITTLE CHILDREN

The ringing phone wrenched me from hard-earned sleep, and I groaned. Late-night calls never brought good news.

I slipped from Greg's arms and grabbed the receiver. "Hello," I mumbled, tugging my cami straight.

"Sheriff, it's Madelyn Kelner down at the hospital. I'm sorry to call so late."

The alarm clock read 3:14. Felt more like 'so early' to me.

"It's okay, Madelyn. What's happening?"

"Ambulance brought Shirley Byerrum in. She tried to avoid a deer and crashed her car into a tree. Looks like she's not going to make it, and she's asking for you."

Odd. Shirley had been the department's file clerk when I was first elected sheriff eleven years ago. I'd let her go pretty soon after. She was too sloppy. And nosy. And she spent half her time in the office playing word games on her computer. The only interaction we'd had since then was her giving me the evil eye every time she saw me. Hard to believe I'd be the last person she'd want to see on this earth.

"All right, Madelyn. I'm on my way."

I threw the blanket onto my husband, who was snoring something fierce. That man could sleep through a train wreck.

"Sheriff," Madelyn said. "You better hurry."

* * * *

Twenty minutes later I hustled into the hospital's emergency entrance. Madelyn emerged from behind the nurse's desk. Her bulging stomach seemed even bigger than when I saw her just a week ago. That baby was going to be a big one.

"She still alive?"

Madelyn nodded, and her auburn bangs brushed her hazel eyes. "Hard to believe with her injuries."

"She lucid?"

"Yep on that, too. And as ornery as ever."

Madelyn pointed to a curtained area by the far wall. I walked over and stepped inside. Shirley was hooked up to several beeping machines. Her wrinkled face was as gray as her hair, and deep purple bruises covered her bird-like arms. She seemed shriveled. A shadow of her former self.

"Shirley," I said softly as I approached her bed. Seeing her like that made me regret all the bad feelings between us.

Her eyes opened, alert. She moved her head slightly, motioning me to come closer.

I grasped the bed's handrail and stood over her. "What is it, Shirley?"

She took a couple shallow breaths. "Sheriff."

"Yes?"

"I've never liked you."

I clamped my mouth shut, biting my tongue. That was Shirley in a nutshell. Even lying on her deathbed, all she could think about was sticking it to me.

She coughed. "But I can't die like this. Not without telling."

Telling?

"Telling what, Shirley?" I shifted closer.

"Those boys. Those missing boys. I know who grabbed 'em."

My breath caught in my chest. Five boys had gone missing in the county over the past two years. The youngest was seven. The oldest, eleven. I'd had many sleepless nights since the disappearances began. We'd never had a single lead. Till now.

"Who, Shirley? Who is it?"

She paused, the corners of her mouth curling up slightly. "Harlow Springer."

"The funeral director?"

I shook my head. The accusation was hard to believe. The man had lived in this county all his life, near on sixty years. He was a member of the Chamber of Commerce. A veteran. He had an easy-going way about him, and was kind and supportive to folks in their time of need. But I'd learned the hard way in this job that people aren't always what they appear to be. Darkness can hide behind a gleaming smile. It only slithers out when you're not looking.

"How do you know?"

"I used to work at the funeral home. Was Harlow's assistant."

"Yeah, I know. Harlow fired you about three months ago. Makes me question your credibility."

Her eyes narrowed. "You want to hear my story or not?"

I nodded.

"One day last fall I forgot my phone in my desk, so after dinner, I drove back to work."

Her breathing was becoming more labored, her voice raspy. God, please don't take her before she's finished.

"He didn't know I was there. Harlow. I saw him carry...the Kinzell boy from the back. Dead. Put him in a casket. Then covered him up with padding." She panted harder. "Then he set Judy Amblyne on top."

I gulped. Could it be true? Kevin Kinzell was the last of the missing boys. He'd disappeared a few weeks before Judy died. Had Harlow really buried Kevin along with Judy? Had he disposed of the four other boys' bodies in the same way? It would explain why we'd never had even a sighting of any of them.

"Damn it, Shirley. Why didn't you call me right then?" If she hadn't been at death's door, I'd have arrested her for obstruction of justice. How could she have kept this monstrous secret?

"Don't look at me like that. I was...too scared. Tiptoed out. Went home. Got drunk. Tried to forget. But I can't forget. Had to tell before I die." She blinked, wincing. "I would've written this secret down in a letter if I had the strength...so I wouldn't have to talk to you. I hate you...and your whole compartment."

She wheezed. "Department. You could stand in a forest and never see what's right below the trees. You're a horrible—"

She started gasping, and the machines changed from beeping to ringing, as if we were in some bizarre version of Las Vegas.

"Shirley? What about the other boys?" I shook her arm. "Shirley!"

Doc Reid and a couple nurses hurried in and shooed me out.

Son of a bitch! I paced around the emergency room for a few minutes, kicking at the linoleum floor with my scuffed boots. I had too many unanswered questions. Finally, Doc Reid came out. I looked up, hopeful.

"I'm sorry, Ellen," he said. "She's gone."

* * * *

I spent the rest of the night in my office, guzzling coffee, thinking things through. If Shirley had told the truth, chances were all those boys were buried in the county cemetery, hidden in other folks' coffins. But which ones? There was no easy way to find out. Harlow could have kept those kids alive for weeks. Months even. Heck, one could still be alive, squirreled away somewhere.

Come eight a.m., I stood waiting outside Judge Nate Irwin's office. I was thankful the judge was an early riser. He raised his gray, caterpillar-like eyebrows in surprise as he came around the corner.

"Morning, Sheriff. What brings you here so early?"

I followed him into his office, closing the door behind us. The judge offered me a chair, but I was too hyped up for that. He sat down behind his battered wooden desk. I leaned over it.

"I need warrants to search Harlow Springer's home and business."

"Springer?" He shifted forward. "What on earth for?"

I told him everything that had happened last night, finishing up with, "I also need a court order to exhume some bodies."

I handed him my applications for the warrants and the court order.

"Some?" He scanned my documents and looked up at me. "Are you kidding? You want a court order to dig up every single body buried in this county in the last two years?"

"No, sir. Just the ones handled by Springer Funeral Home. I believe I said that in my application."

He scowled. "Which is nearly everybody, as you well know. Springer gets, what, eighty percent of the body business in these parts?"

"Yes, sir."

I actually only wanted permission to exhume Judy Amblyne's coffin, for now. But Judge Irwin never liked to give me everything I wanted, so I'd asked for more. A lot more. Besides, if things turned out as I expected, I'd be back here soon enough asking for all those coffins anyway. Might as well get him used to the idea.

The judge picked up his pen. Pointed it at me. "I sign this, and we both might as well start packing up our offices. The good people of Median County will hand us our hats come next election day."

He was probably right. Greg had made that very point when I spoke to him on the phone an hour ago. Digging up the dead— especially so many of them—would be indecent. But this search had to be done.

"Sure, they'll be mad at first, Judge. But once we find those missing kids, they'll calm down." I hoped.

"You certain those boys' bodies are hidden in some of those coffins?"

"Yes, sir. I trust my source."

Irwin harrumphed and settled back to read my affidavit, which I'd included with my applications. It detailed my conversation last night with Shirley. The judge knew that she'd worked as a funeral assistant for Springer till January, when they had their non-mutual parting of the ways. I hoped he wouldn't hold it against me now.

He finished reading and looked up. "What makes you think you can trust Shirley Byerrum? She was meaner than a rattle-snake. Hated half the town, especially kids. And she could hold a grudge longer than anyone I know. She was probably making all this up about Harlow to spite him for firing her. And to set you up, too. Exhuming these bodies will make you oh so popular around here, especially if your investigation proves fruitless. Not to mention the cost to the taxpayers."

I swallowed hard. I had considered Shirley's bitterness toward Harlow and me all last night, but, ultimately, I had to follow this lead, no matter the consequences.

"I don't think she was lying, Judge. It was a death-bed confession. People don't lie right before they meet their maker."

That may not have been true about Shirley, given her general nastiness. But I had a feeling she was right, that digging up those coffins was the key to finding those missing boys.

The judge shook his head. "I can't do it. I can't let you exhume all those folks. You're probably talking about fifty people."

"Judge—"

He sliced his hand through the air, cutting me off. "But here's what I will do. I'll give you your warrants to search Springer's house and business. And I'll let you exhume Judy Amblyne. If you find the Kinzell boy's remains in her coffin, like Shirley said, then we'll talk about expanding the search." He modified my requested court order and signed it, as well as my warrant applications. "You best tell her husband first. Don't want him finding out through the grapevine."

"Yes, sir." I grabbed the papers and hightailed it out of there before the judge could change his mind. Or figure out that he'd given me exactly what I'd wanted.

* * * *

We executed the warrants immediately. I searched Harlow's house myself with part of my team. My deputy, Jackson, supervised the search of the funeral home. Neither search turned up anything. But they sure riled Harlow up. I'd never seen him so mad. I assigned two of my officers to follow him for the foreseeable future—one all day, the other all night—to make sure he didn't dispose of any evidence or try to run away. More than a little discouraged, I returned to my office to eat lunch and discuss next steps with Jackson.

I could only recall one time a body had been exhumed in the county. It had been about twenty-five years ago, when I was on patrol, so I wasn't sure about the procedure. Jackson hadn't even been on the force then, but, thankfully, while I'd been with Judge Irwin, Jackson had been busy researching our state's exhumation rules and had made a print-out of what we'd need to do.

"Okay," I said, swallowing another bite of my turkey on rye. "Let's go over the list. We need a backhoe, three diggers, and a coffin key from the cemetery."

"Check." Jackson sipped his water, keeping his brown eyes trained on me.

"A pickup with a hoist attached to haul up the coffin and vault."

"Check."

"The medical examiner to take possession of Kevin."

"Check."

"The state health officer to…do whatever it is he does in these circumstances." I finished off my sandwich.

"Check. Assuming we find Kevin, the health officer will assist with moving the coffin to the M.E.'s office so we can do a thorough search for Harlow's prints and DNA and such, without causing a health issue. He'll also bring all the protective clothing we'll need. Um, boss, you have some mustard…" He tapped his upper lip.

"Thanks." I wiped my mouth with my napkin, then tossed it and the brown paper sandwich bag in the trash. "We should set up a tent to shield the coffin from any gawkers."

"Check."

"Is that it?"

"I think so." Jackson pushed away half of his tuna sandwich. "I'll take care of all of this, boss, and arrange for the exhumation to occur ASAP."

I stood, pulling my keys from my pocket. "Thanks. I guess that leaves the fun part for me."

He grimaced. "Give my regards to Mr. Amblyne."

"And the Kinzells. They'll be my second stop. I can't let them hear about this from anyone but me."

* * * *

John Amblyne lived in the northeast part of the county, on about twenty-five acres of land, mostly fields, with a large stand of ponderosa pine behind the house. While I drove out to his place, I planned how I'd approach him. I needed him to agree to Judy's exhumation. If he decided to fight it in court, Lord knows how long the delay would be. I had to find those kids now. They deserved a better resting place than they'd received from Harlow Springer.

I'd only been to the Amblyne house once before, the day Judy died last fall. I'd been about ten minutes away when the ambulance call went out, so I drove over to see if I could help. Unfortunately no one could. Judy's heart attack had been massive. She'd died before she hit the floor. I'd found John kneeling over her body in the living room, whispering to her. He'd appeared completely lost. They'd been married about forty-five years, and I doubted he knew how to live without her. Now, as I drove up the driveway, it seemed I'd been right. Weeds had sprouted around the porch. The yard was full of their dog, Buster's, waste. And the paint on the front of the yellow house was peeling. John had clearly been letting things go. I parked by his dirty pickup and went to the door.

I knocked, and barking erupted from inside. When John opened the door, Buster stood slobbering, happy to see me. John smiled, too. He looked older than I remembered. And far older than I knew him to be. He'd retired from the postal service a couple years ago, when he turned sixty-five, but he appeared at least ten years older than that now. His beard, formerly grizzled, had turned all gray. The bald spot on his head had grown. And he had deep lines etched into his forehead. He and Judy hadn't had any kids, so now it was just him and the dog and a whole lot of time on his hands.

"Sheriff," he said. "What can I do for you?"

"Hello, Mr. Amblyne. I'm sorry to bother you, but we need to speak about something important. May I come in?"

He paused a moment, then pulled the door open wide. "Me and Buster don't usually have visitors."

I stepped inside onto a sisal rug and went into the living room. The interior of the house seemed better cared for. Things were tidy, if a bit dusty.

"Can I get you something to drink?" he asked. "Or some cookies?"

I desperately wanted coffee, but I shook my head. "No thanks." I needed to get through this.

I sat on the couch, the cushion sagging beneath me. A framed photo stood on the scarred end table to my left. John and Judy, all smiles, having a picnic. The picture must have been taken a while back, before Judy started having so much trouble walking and taking the stairs. John sat beside me, and Buster curled into a brown ball by our feet. "Mr. Amblyne, there's no easy way for me to say this, so I'm just going to say it."

His eyes widened a bit.

"You know about those five missing boys?"

He nodded. "What about them?"

"I have a witness who says that the body of one of those boys has been hidden in your wife's coffin."

"What?" His Adam's apple bulged.

"I need you to keep this between us for now. But an accusation has been made—a credible accusation—that someone at the funeral home put one of the boys into Judy's coffin, under some padding, and then set Judy on top. We need to know if that's true. So, I'm very sorry, but we have to exhume your wife's body. To find that boy. To give his parents some closure. I'm sure you can understand. We'll treat her with the utmost respect."

"You want to pull Judy up out of the ground?" He shook his head. "No. No!"

I scooted toward him, grasped his hands. They felt leathery and worn. "I know you don't have any children of your own, Mr. Amblyne, but I'm sure you can understand how this boy's parents have been suffering and why we have to do this."

"Who are they?"

"The Kinzells."

John pulled away, turned, and gazed out the window. A bunch of Canada geese were flying in a V formation over his grove of trees, heading back north. He sat quietly for a few moments before he faced me, paler than he'd been before.

"A nice family," he said. "They were on my route. I saw their boy sometimes. On Saturdays he'd run down their driveway to get their mail straight from me. He always had such a spark about him." He paused. "You won't hurt Judy, will you?"

"No. We'll be as gentle and careful as we can."

"You'll just check if that boy's under her and then rebury her right away?"

I nodded, feeling guilty. That was only true if we didn't find Kevin. If we did, the whole coffin, including Judy and Kevin, would have to be removed for investigation. But I feared he'd go to court to try to stop the exhumation if I told him that.

He sat quietly for a good half-minute. "Do I have to be there?" he finally said.

"No."

"Good. I don't think I could stand seeing that. Will you let me know, though, when it's scheduled for, in case I change my mind?"

"Of course."

I squeezed his hand once more, patted the dog's head, and left. I was so glad he wasn't going to put up a fight. And even happier that he didn't want to attend the exhumation. As much as he couldn't stand watching it, I didn't think I could stand seeing him go through that. The poor man had already been through enough.

* * * *

Three days later, I sat in my office as the first rays of dawn shone through my window. For the past hour, I'd been staring at smudged photos of Timmy Garmer, Kevin Kinzell, and the three other missing boys. I knew every sandy hair on Timmy's head. Every freckle on Kevin's sunburned cheeks. I'd looked at Timmy's picture so many times in the last two years, it was hard to believe that finally, *finally*, we had a break. Timmy had been ten when his parents reported him missing. He was the first one to disappear.

"Boss." Jackson knocked on my open office door. "I just spoke to the health officer. She's driving straight to the cemetery with the medical examiner. They should be there shortly. And the diggers and equipment are already on site. You ready to go?"

"Yep." I set the photos back in my file and closed it. Then I stood, my left knee creaking as it often did ever since I tackled a fleeing suspect a few years back. "Is the tent up?"

"Yeah, I checked last night on my way home. Mrs. Amblyne will be afforded the most privacy we can give her." Jackson stepped into the room, his pants sagging off his lean frame.

I smiled. I could always count on Jackson to do things right.

"Boss," he said as I grabbed my jacket. "Why didn't you question Harlow first, before going through all this?"

"What's he gonna say? 'Oh, yes, I abducted all those boys, did unspeakable things to them, and then stuffed their bodies in other folks' coffins.' No. I want the evidence first. Then we'll watch him try to squirm out of it."

He nodded. "Plus, Shirley mighta been lying."

I exhaled a big breath. "Yeah, there's that."

Jackson and I drove south on Route Eighteen separately in case we each needed to attend to different matters after we dug up Judy. I rolled down my window. Spring had come. The air smelled fresh and green, and violets lined the countryside on both sides of the road. Their beauty made this whole business feel even more unseemly.

I wished there'd been a way we could have kept the exhumation a secret, in case we were wrong. But by yesterday, word had gotten around, as I'd feared it would. The whole county was upset all over again, especially the parents of those missing kids. If we found Kevin's remains today, they'd all be devastated. One couple simply wanted closure, and would, sadly, welcome knowing what likely had happened to their son. But the rest, including Kevin's parents, still believed their boys were alive somewhere and one day they'd come home.

Sighing, I turned into the gravel lot beside the cemetery. Jackson pulled in behind me. About fifty yards in, a large white tent covered what I assumed was Judy Amblyne's grave. Several people stood near it, looking out toward my rig. The Kinzells and the Garmers and four of the other parents. And Harlow. He definitely shouldn't be here. And there was a reporter from the local paper, too. Dang. I had really wanted to keep this from turning into a circus. I couldn't identify the others standing by the tent because they all were wearing white coveralls, surgical masks, and gloves. I assumed they were the diggers, the M.E., and the state and cemetery officials, though considering the location, they could've been a bunch of weird-looking ghosts.

I steeled my shoulders and opened my vehicle door. Show time.

* * * *

Soon the backhoe broke the ground, and the diggers grabbed shovels and began work. At first I stood watching, wishing my coveralls had pockets, but after a while I started pacing. I hoped we'd find Kevin's body. And I hoped we wouldn't. The optimistic part of me wanted those parents to be right, that their sons were still alive out there somewhere.

I peeked outside the tent. Before the work had begun, my officers had moved the parents, Harlow, and the reporter to the parking lot, where they couldn't compromise the investigation. Kevin's parents looked sad. Timmy's looked hopeful. Harlow simply looked angry. And the reporter appeared frustrated. I didn't give a damn about her.

After about an hour of digging, the concrete vault containing Judy's coffin finally emerged. The workers dug by hand around the vault's edges, making enough room to attach a steel cable to the sides. That cable was fastened to a long boom, which was attached to the hoist in a pickup truck parked on a path just outside the tent. Ron, the cemetery official, pushed aside the tent flap and signaled to the guy in the pickup. He started the engine and slowly began moving down the path, pulling the heavy vault up behind him.

The activity stirred the parking lot crowd. They all swarmed forward, trying to get a better look. My officers held them back.

When the vault cleared the grave, it was set down with a thud on a grassy spot nearby, still inside the tent. One of the diggers grabbed a sledgehammer and started pounding away on the vault's side.

"There's no other way to open that thing?" I asked Ron.

"Nope," he said. "You have to break it open."

God, I hoped they wouldn't smash the coffin.

At last enough damage had been done to the vault lid, and the workers used a crowbar to lift it off. My adrenaline surged as the coffin came into sight. Oak. Dirt covered some of its rounded lid. I wanted to rush to it. Pry it open. But the coffin was still in the vault. I had to wait while the diggers threaded straps underneath the coffin and lugged it out.

They probably were working pretty fast, but my patience was shot. I started drumming my hand against my thigh until, finally, they set the coffin on the grass. Jackson and I charged forward. Ron unlocked the lid covering the lower half of the coffin, then the lid covering the upper half. The seconds it took while he raised the halves felt like forever.

I'd known gasses would escape when they opened the coffin—that's one reason why we had to wear surgical masks—but I hadn't expected the smell to be so sickening. I stepped back as the stench of rotting eggs hit me. Then, swallowing bile that was rising in my throat, I looked down at Judy. She was pretty-well preserved, except for the bits of mold growing on her face and hands. I'd been to a lot of crime scenes before, including folks who'd come to their end in violent ways, but seeing Judy like that still made me cringe. I'd never forget that image.

She lay on white padding, her head nestled on a white pillow. I nodded at Jackson. He slid his hands under Judy and rolled her stiff body sideways. I held my breath, my hands nearly shaking, as I grabbed the padding and began lifting it. In that moment, I didn't know what to pray for anymore, finding Kevin, or not finding him.

I pushed the padding all the way back and blinked. "Jesus."

The coffin was empty.

I dropped the padding and stepped back. *That bitch. That lying bitch.* I hoped Shirley Byerrum was burning in hell. Greg had warned me not to trust her. Reminded me how often she lied and how she liked to trick people, making you believe she meant one thing when she really meant another.

Jackson rolled Judy back down. "You can't blame yourself, boss. You said it the other day: We had to check."

He was right, but that didn't make it any easier. As Jackson closed the coffin, I stepped forward, angry. So angry. I slammed my fist against the coffin's lid, and a hollow sound rang out. Jackson and I stared at each other while the medical examiner gasped.

"Did that sound hollow to you?" I asked.

Jackson nodded several times. "Yeah."

I stepped to the head of the coffin and knocked on it repeatedly, moving toward the foot. *Solid wood. Solid wood. Solid wood.* And then, when I knocked on the lower half of the lid, there it was again. That hollow sound.

"Does that sound normal?" I asked.

"Nope, boss. It sure doesn't."

Could Kevin be hidden in the lid, I wondered. And just as quickly, I knew that he could—if he were in pieces. I smothered the urge to punch something hard as Jackson and I began looking at the lower half of the lid, feeling it all over, trying to find a way to get inside it. Nothing. We lifted both halves of the lid again. Examined the lower half from the underside. Nothing. There had to be a way in. There had to be.

I pulled the lid's lower half closed again. Wait a second. What was that on the inside edge? The section you could only see if the bottom half of the lid was closed and the top half was open. A rectangular indentation ran most of the edge's length, and to the left of the indentation, there was a circular groove in the wood. A button.

My heart racing, I reached out and pressed it. A drawer

sprang open right beside the button. A folded piece of paper lay on black velvet. I picked it up and silently began reading the shaky, cursive handwriting.

My darling Judy,

I love and miss you more than words can say. For all these years, you've been my conscience. You've helped me be the person I wanted to be. You knew about my weakness and loved me anyway.

I never meant for you to learn that I slipped up. I've had too much free time since retiring. The urges have been over-whelming. I never imagined you'd brave the staircase down to the basement ever again, that you'd find any of them. I'm so sorry.

I'll live the rest of my life with the utter shame of what I've done. Of what I am. Of how I upset you so much that your heart literally stopped beating. Last night I buried the Kinzell boy under the trees out back with the others. I swear on my life I'll try not to act on my sickness again and to be the man you always thought I could be. I'll love and miss you until my dying hour, and I'll pray we'll meet again someday.

John

Holy shit. I looked up. Everyone was staring at me.

"What's it say, boss?"

I couldn't tell him with so many people standing around. "Jackson, we need the coffin fingerprinted, especially the inside of this drawer. And it needs to be checked for hairs, fiber, DNA. The whole gamut. We'll have to check this letter, too, but first I need to show it to Judge Irwin. Hand me an evidence bag."

He did, questioning me with his eyes. I slipped the letter inside the bag. "I'm leaving you in charge here. I'll fill you in later."

I ran out of the tent, ripping off my coveralls, mask, and gloves as I dashed to my rig. The parents and the reporter started moving my way, calling out questions. I didn't really have time to stop, but I owed the parents, especially the Kinzells, answers, however brief.

I slowed and turned. "We didn't find Kevin."

"I told you so!" Harlow said, while Kevin's mother burst into tears, and his father said, "I knew it. My son's alive somewhere."

It broke my heart to know otherwise. But I couldn't say anything at that point.

The other parents advanced, shouting questions. "I'm sorry," I said. "I can't talk now. Something's come up. It's best if you all go on home."

"What's come up, Sheriff?" the reporter asked.

"Not now."

I hurried to my rig, motioning for my officers to follow. When we got away from prying ears, I doled out assignments. One officer would stay in the parking lot, keeping folks out of the tent. One would help Jackson collect the evidence. The rest would drive to Amblyne's house and wait till I joined them.

"Why?" asked Shep, one of my officers.

"No time to explain. But don't let John Amblyne go near the trees behind the house. If you see him head out back, stop him and bring him in for questioning. And if you see him leave, someone follow him, and let me know what's going on."

"What about Springer?" Shep asked. "I thought I needed to tail him."

"That's not necessary anymore. You all have your assignments. Go!"

I drove as fast as I safely could back to town. During the drive, I called Judge Irwin. Said I had to see him. It was urgent. I couldn't explain over an open line. When I got to his office, he was waiting for me. He waved me inside and shut the door.

"Did you find the boy?"

"No," I said, pulling on latex gloves I'd grabbed from my rig. "I found this instead." I removed the letter from its paper evidence bag, unfolded it, and set it on his desk. "Read it, but don't touch it. It's evidence."

While Irwin read the letter, I tried to remain still. John Amblyne. As a mailman, he could have known all these kids. They would have trusted him. He'd said Kevin used to run to him on Saturdays to get the family's mail. And he'd offered me cookies when I was at his house. That's not something you typically offer adults. But children—cookies could easily lure them in, as could a cute dog like Buster.

The judge finished reading. "Son of a bitch." He knit his eyebrows together so they looked like one. "Any chance Shirley forged this note?"

Any chance? After the lies she'd told about Harlow, I'd put nothing past that old biddy. But I needed a warrant in case the letter was real.

"It rings true, Judge. We just need to search Amblyne's land to know for sure."

"All right," he said. "I'm writing a warrant to search his house, truck, and land." He looked up at me. "Go find those boys."

A half-hour later, I zoomed up Amblyne's driveway. His pickup was gone. Shit.

"Shep," I called, jumping out of my rig. "Any sign of Amblyne?"

"No, ma'am." He hurried over. "Haven't seen anyone since we got here."

I called my dispatcher. Put out a BOLO for Amblyne. I didn't want him stopped or approached. I simply wanted to know his location. Then I told my officers what was going on, and we ran up to Amblyne's door. I pounded on it, announced myself and the warrant. Buster started barking madly, but otherwise things remained quiet. I let Shep kick the door in. He liked doing things like that.

Once inside, my men fanned out. I headed down to the basement, gun in hand, in case Amblyne was hiding down there. As I descended the last steep step, I craned my neck, ready to react. But no one jumped out at me. No missing children. No Amblyne. Slowly I checked out the whole level. It was mostly a large storage area filled with tools, boxes, and old furniture. In the back I found a windowless room with a lock on the open door and a cot inside. Where Amblyne must have kept the boys, though I found no direct evidence of that.

My radio squawked. Amblyne's pickup had been spotted outside the Methodist church in town. I found Shep, told him to supervise the search of the grounds once the cadaver dog arrived, and I sped off toward town.

Amblyne knew we were digging up Judy this morning. He must have worried we'd find the note. What was he doing at church? Seeking sanctuary? I gripped the steering wheel tight. There was no place he could hide from me.

The winding county roads seemed longer than usual as I sped to the church. Finally I pulled up, right behind Amblyne's pickup. I reminded myself to keep cool and headed inside. I spotted Amblyne immediately, sitting alone in a pew near the front.

"John." I stood behind him and put on my best smile.

"Sheriff." He looked up, wide-eyed. "What happened with Judy?"

I sat down beside him, forcing him to move over a bit. "We didn't find Kevin."

He exhaled loudly.

"I'm really disappointed." I stared at the large cross in front of us. "The Kinzells are religious, you know. Like Judy was. Like you apparently are. I doubt they'll be able to find peace in this life, or the next one, without answers. Someone out there knows what happened to Kevin and the rest of those boys. I wonder what Judy would say to that person."

I turned and looked square at Amblyne. He stared at his lap. I waited a full minute, but my guilt trip wasn't working so I switched to Plan B. "We did find something interesting this morning. A letter. In Judy's coffin."

John's head snapped back up. "You promised you would only look under Judy. You weren't supposed to open that drawer."

And just like that, I had the confirmation I needed that he'd written the letter, not Shirley. "How'd you know the letter was in a drawer, John?"

He sputtered as I stood, cuffed him, and read him his rights. My first arrest in a church. I hoped it'd be my last.

While we were driving to the station, my phone rang. Shep. "Good news?" I asked.

"If you could call it that," he said. "The dog arrived right after you left, Sheriff. Only took her a few minutes sniffing through those pine trees before she lay down. So we started digging right there and found human bones. Small ones."

Damn it! They'd found the remains under the trees out back. The trees Amblyne had stared at when I told him I believed Kevin's body was hidden in his wife's coffin. The bastard had been staring at the boys' actual resting place the whole time. "You be careful with all that evidence, Shep. I'll be there as soon as I can."

I disconnected and looked in the rearview mirror. "It's all over, John. We've found 'em."

That's when I saw a tear roll down his cheek. "I'm sorry. But I've refrained since Judy died. And I tried not to do it before then. I just couldn't help myself."

Every pervert I'd ever met had the same sorry excuse. It never washed with me.

"You think saying you're sorry makes everything all better? You're going to rot in prison and then, the good Lord willing, in hell. You'll never see Judy again."

That last part was harsh, I know, but I couldn't help *myself.*

By noon, Amblyne had written a full confession and had been booked. I went to visit each of the boys' parents that afternoon, filling them in. It was the hardest thing I'd done in my whole life. I cursed Amblyne for it. They did, too.

Before heading home for the day, I stopped back at my office to ensure Amblyne was locked up tight. All I wanted to do next was fall into Greg's arms and forget. Forget all of this.

Forget…

What had Shirley said? Her last words? I sat at my desk and pulled out a copy of the affidavit I'd drafted just after she'd died, where I'd tried to get down exactly what she'd said: "I would've written this secret down in a letter if I had the strength…so I wouldn't have to talk to you. I hate you…and your whole compartment. Department. You could stand in a forest and never see what's right below the trees." Words jumped out at me. *Letter. Secret compartment. What's right below the trees.* God damn. Greg had been right. She'd been tricking me. With her final words, Shirley had given me the clues to find the letter *and* told me where the bodies were buried.

A knock on my office door startled me. I glanced up.

"Judge Irwin. I'm surprised to see you here."

"Mind if I come in?" he asked.

"Please do."

He shut the door behind him, then sat in my guest chair. "I heard."

"No surprise there," I said. "The county grapevine works fast."

"Well, I'm glad that Harlow's cleared. I had a hard time believing he could've been capable of these atrocities."

"But you could believe it of Amblyne?"

He shrugged. "It's hard to believe it of anybody."

"Yeah." I told him about Shirley, about the hidden meaning behind her last words. "She was pretty crafty. If we hadn't found the letter, I would've been blamed for causing anguish and wasting taxpayer funds. I would've looked incompetent. Probably would have lost re-election, which Shirley would have loved. And Harlow would've had a black mark on him for the rest of his life. Everyone would've always wondered about him."

"But you did find the letter."

"Yeah, which served Shirley's purposes, too. Turns out she also hated Amblyne 'cause he lost some of her mail at one point." He'd mentioned it during his interrogation, once he found out Shirley had been my source. I guess he hoped I'd sympathize with him, given my history with Shirley. He'd been wrong.

The judge whistled. "Shirley was a piece of work. No matter what happened, she got what she wanted."

"Yep. Hard to believe she knew what Amblyne was up to and didn't tell anyone. She left every boy in this county at risk. What kind of person does that?"

The judge leaned forward. "Ellen, I wouldn't focus too much on Shirley's swiss-cheese soul. I'd focus on the fact that she helped you stop a predator and get a lot of people some much-needed closure."

"You're right. I hadn't thought of it that way. In the end, Shirley was awful helpful." I laughed. "She was buried just yesterday. She must be rolling over in her grave."

"We could check," the judge said with a twinkle in his eye. "That's an exhumation I'll approve."

❧

More than a decade ago I visited a funeral home, gathering information for a novel that ultimately died after a dozen chapters. One thing in particular from that visit stuck with me—the secret drawer that some caskets have. As soon as I learned about the drawer, I knew I'd have to use it somehow, someway, in my writing. Well, it certainly took a while, but good things can take time to coalesce. Thank you to the Robert A. Pumphrey Funeral Home in Bethesda, Maryland, for eliciting the spark that ultimately turned into "Suffer the Little Children." (I wish I could personally thank the man who gave me the tour, but my notes, including his name, were lost in my last move.) And thank you to Gary Downer of Money & King Funeral Home in Vienna, Virginia, for letting me pick his brain about exhumation and all kinds of stuff that many people would probably think is gross, but I thought were way cool.